SHORT SCI-FI ADVENTURES

LANCE ERLICK

Finlee Augare Books (Chicago)

"Regina Shen: Salvage" copyright © 2015 by Lance Erlick
"Unintended Rebel" copyright © 2015 by Lance Erlick
"She-Devil Rocks" copyright © 2015 by Lance Erlick
"Maiden Voyage" copyright © 2014 by Lance Erlick
"Watching You" copyright © 2013 by Lance Erlick
"Regina Shen: Into the Storm" copyright © 2015 by Lance Erlick

Finlee Augare Books, Chicago, IL
ISBN: 978-1-943080-19-9 (print)
ISBN: 978-1-943080-20-5 (e-book)
Library of Congress Control Number: 2016902682

Printed in the United States of America

TABLE OF CONTENTS

REGINA SHEN: SALVAGE...1
UNINTENDED REBEL 23
SHE-DEVIL ROCKS...47
MAIDEN VOYAGE 81
WATCHING YOU 107
REGINA SHEN: INTO THE STORM 121
OTHER STORIES BY LANCE ERLICK i
ABOUT THE AUTHOR..iii

REGINA SHEN: SALVAGE
(Prequel to Regina Shen series)

Richmond Swamps, October ACM 295

Gale force winds howled. Lightning flashed beyond cracks in the cellar door above us. Like a drum beat, the door banged violently against its latches, threatening to tear loose. Rain streamed through the edges of the frame into our small, earthen shelter. Already water was up to my knees and we were hanging from the steel frame that held up the ceiling.

Colleen clung to me in a death grip. My eleven-year-old sister had a bad case of the storm tremors that left her paralyzed in fear. I felt the urge, yet focused on her as I adjusted the harness that held us mostly above water.

"Don't let go, Regina," Colleen said through clattering teeth.

I gave her a squeeze. "It'll be okay, sis." *Hold on a little longer.*

Her head nodded acknowledgement, yet she trembled. Last year we'd found neighbors who had drowned in a similar cellar. Their pit had filled with rainwater. When they tried to escape, a tree that had fallen over the opening blocked them.

Colleen's breathing grew shallow. Her pulse raced. She had to be exhausted from shivering in the heat, though she hadn't whimpered. She didn't want me to feel sorry for her. With each storm, she got worse. There was no getting used to them; no immunization eased the terror they brought. What kept me going was my need to protect my sister. I held her tight for me as much as for her.

1

Across the hollowed out pit we called a cellar, Mom flashed a light. She checked ropes securing what food and bedding we'd brought down. Water was above her waist and had soaked our supplies, yet the ropes held. She turned out the light plunging us back into darkness.

Waiting through the third hurricane of the season, I couldn't help wondering what it was like beyond the Great Barrier Wall and whether I might make it on the other side. That was if I survived this and found a way over the Wall. After all, the coastal swamps and scattered islands were the only home I'd known.

The World Federation had built the Wall to hold back rising seas from abrupt climate change. And to create a place outside the Federation to dump outcasts like my mom before Colleen and I were born. When I'd asked Mom about what happened, she refused to talk about the past. "Use your energy to stay alive and do your best," she'd said.

Lightning struck nearby. Wood splintered above us. The cellar door held, but I worried. I said a prayer for the storm to spare us and realized how pathetic I sounded. Praying to the Grand Old Dames who condemned us to this slice of drenched islands was a waste of energy better focused on survival.

The door banged in an unnerving rhythm, weakening the latches. Then as suddenly as the storm began, it simmered down. It didn't intend to kill us this time, merely to wear us down and test our resolve. Every act of survival was protest against what the Federation had done to us.

Winds ceased torturing the door, but calm was as unnerving as the storm. I held my breath, hoping this wasn't the eye of the hurricane with more to come. Rain slowed to a trickle and stopped. Our faded green canvas clothes were soaked and humidity wouldn't let us dry out, but I breathed easier.

Light poked through cracks in the cellar door above us, the first sign of hope in hours. The storm was ending. In a few months, winter, such as it was, would bring an end to these storms. It had in the past, though with temperatures rising, hurricane season kept growing longer and more intense.

"You okay, Mom?" I called out across the dark shadows.

"Never better," Mom said in a steady voice intended to calm Colleen. She turned on a flashlight so we could see. "Stake claim to our property."

2

The storm was bad enough, but scavengers were like Biblical locusts, swarming the land, stripping it bare, and taking what little survived.

I unstrapped myself from the harness anchored to rusted steel pipes that went some twenty feet into the ground below us. When I dropped, the water in the cellar was above my waist. I unfastened Colleen and eased her onto a nearby ledge. Three years younger, she was much shorter, and I didn't want her to panic.

She hugged me tight. "Thanks, Regina," she whispered.

The words carried dread that I might abandon her to the storm. *Never.*

Colleen let go and eased her way around the pit to Mom, who was inspecting our belongings. Mom gave her a quick hug and pushed her toward the cellar door. We had work to do.

"Come on, sis," I said after I unlatched the cellar door.

I pushed open the door, grabbed my crossbow, and pulled myself up to our wind-whipped world. The river channels frothed with tension. Tree limbs scattered around our small island: firewood for cooking. Our orange and apple trees had shed much of their fruit across the clearing. A hint of citrus filled the air as if the storm had swept away our usual dank swampy aromas.

"Gather what you can," I whispered and ran toward our water system.

The roof had blown off our water tanks and lay under fallen tree branches. The river-water tank was on its side with the lid missing. Water spilled onto the mud. A two-inch gash poked through the side of the tank. I wasn't sure if we could repair it and I couldn't see the lid.

Dreading the loss of clean water, I examined the fresh-water tank, which remained upright. The float showed three-quarters full, but the ground was so soaked, I couldn't be sure there wasn't a leak. At least I spotted no gaping holes and the lid protected the precious contents.

We would have to be water-frugal until Mom and I could fix the river-water tank and make sure the water purifiers worked.

Nearby, roof timbers had ripped off our cabin. The walls were battered yet our home stood. Checking the inside and the rest of our possessions would have to wait. We had to make sure scavengers knew we could get by.

While Colleen gathered fruit, I hurried down to our boat dock. I

3

slung my crossbow over my shoulder so I could use both hands to steady myself down slippery rocks covered in topsoil the storm tried to wash away.

The water had risen five feet and broke in waves over our rocky shores. The river had swamped our docking cove. Thankfully, Mom and I had secured her skiff's mooring rope to trees on what had been dry ground. Now the boat was in the channel. Floating was good. Slow leaks we could fix, but a gash or shattered frame would doom us.

A power boat motored up the channel toward our island. Eyeing our skiff, scavengers in green-canvas rags looked for anything they could use. I grabbed our boat's nylon rope and hauled it in.

The scavengers drew closer. I wrapped the rope around my left arm, pulled my crossbow from my shoulder, and removed the safety. One of the scavengers was a girl a year older than me whom I'd bartered with on occasion. I aimed the bow. *Stay away.*

An older scavenger woman who didn't look to be the girl's mother waved in a friendly manner and motored closer. She scanned our island. "You survived?"

It sounded more like a question than a statement of fact. I had the impression she was disappointed. After all, wood and supplies were scarce on this side of the Wall.

I steadied my bow. "We have food, water, and the skiff," I said as proof that we could carry on. I had no doubt the woman would have taken those if I hadn't been there.

The motorboat moved away. "Good luck," the scavenger woman said. She didn't offer to help us rebuild.

A gun cocked behind me. I turned to see Mom atop a rocky ledge with Colleen at her side. She held her rifle aimed at the horizon. I followed her line of sight to a bounty boat across the channel. Two women in brown alligator leather used binoculars to scan us.

Bounty hunters were outcasts like us who picked up lost girls during and after storms. They made their living by selling their captives into slavery beyond the Wall to fill jobs Federation citizens didn't want like mine and farm laborers. I'd lost a friend last year when bounty hunters got to her before I could.

It had been that way all my life. Neighbors barely survived on shrinking islands, all due to crimes they or their ancestors may have committed in the misty past. *But why must the sins of the mothers fall upon their daughters?* After all, Colleen and I were born here.

The bounty hunters across the channel watched me reel in the nylon rope and tie our skiff to a sturdy tree. I was not about to let them take Colleen or me, despite the promise of shelter and meals beyond the Wall. I didn't trust their lies.

The Federation, and their police dogs, the Department of Antiquities, didn't want us outcasts to know that before they took over, the lands around Richmond had been fertile instead of swamps. Our dwindling island had once been the top of a tree-covered hill.

Over the past few centuries, abrupt climate change had altered so much, and it was the job of Antiquities agents to see that nothing from the past surfaced. Yet the sunken Richmond ruins all around us revealed secrets if we held on long enough and knew where to search.

Out in the channel, the bounty boat and the scavengers disappeared behind a nearby island to prey on other families. I worried about neighbors and friends, yet if I didn't help Mom, we wouldn't have a home.

As I secured our skiff, I spotted a leak that needed a weld. Still, a leaky skiff was better than none. Nearby was my log-boat, which I'd carved out of a fallen tree-trunk and made big enough for me and my sister. I'd left it strapped to a tree above the water. Satisfied that we had boats, I headed uphill.

While I thrived on learning about our forbidden past, I cursed my photographic memory, which made me a freak in a world forbidden to read books. This memory refused to let me forget illegal books I'd salvaged that told of the follies of the past. I couldn't fathom knowing how to prevent abrupt climate change and not acting. Yet that was my conclusion after reading books by Lamella Marshall, written in what she called the late twenty-first century, some three-hundred years ago. She'd written a complete history of her time, while climate ran amuck.

From the clearing atop our island, I scanned the channels on all sides. Another scavenger crew moved down river, to where storm surges would have been more devastating. Since we all lived off what we salvaged, it was hard to blame them, yet I did. *Salvage the depths. Don't steal from neighbors.*

I discovered our water-tank lid entangled in bushes. I pulled it free and rolled it toward the water system. While Colleen picked up fallen branches for firewood, I joined Mom by the six-foot-tall aluminum river-water tank.

"We can fix it," she said, pointing to a gash in the seam.

I nodded and ran into our cabin. The kitchen table lay shattered in the corner, the wood in splinters. Bed frames remained nailed to the floor. We'd taken the rest of the bedding into the cellar, where it lay soaked. The wood-burning stove was on its side.

In the back of the cabin, I located a latched compartment beneath the floor from which I grabbed tubes of polymer paste we'd salvaged from the depths. Most of the paste had hardened, but if we cut into the tubes, some had malleable material to plug the water-tank hole. I grabbed two round aluminum strips and ran out to the water system.

Mom helped Colleen build a fire with damp wood in a wheeled barrow so they could move the fire under the tank. I climbed into the water container, cut polymer shavings over the gash, and scooped out a dollop of goo.

The fire had me feverish. Fumes from the polymer choked my throat as the material oozed into the seam. While Mom used tongs to place a circle of aluminum beneath the hole, I spread more material and moved away to keep my sweat from contaminating the weld.

When the polymer began to ooze from the heat, I applied a circle of aluminum above the opening, used my knife handle to press it down, and hoped it would hold. Then I climbed out and collapsed onto the wet grass.

While we waited for the seam to cool, we made repairs to the roof and walls of our cabin to provide shelter for the night. Then the three of us pushed the river-water tank upright and reattached the purifier's pipes.

Using a rusted bicycle frame, I pumped muddy water from the nearby channel into the tank. After the tank was half-full, and not leaking, I helped Mom reattach the tank's lid and make sure the burners would draw sterilized water into the fresh tank.

By the time we finished, I was exhausted, yet worried about my salvage partner. "I'm going to check on Magdalena."

"Not until we've finished repairs," Mom said. Her eyes narrowed. "Not with bounty hunters and scavengers out."

"I'll be extra careful," I said.

"Not now."

There was no arguing when Mom set her mind like this, but I couldn't focus. Magdalena lived in the outer channels, where storm surges were rougher.

She was the closest I had to a friend. I'd skipped two grades in the only remaining school the Federation hadn't closed, where Mom had bartered dearly for Colleen and me to attend. It was hard to make friends with older classmates or those my age in lower grades. Magdalena didn't mind. She was my age, a good diver, and helped me salvage from the drowned ruins of Richmond.

I wished we had those simple twenty-first century communicators. But finding working units was hard, and there were no towers or hubs in the swamps. Besides, Antiquities agents could track signals. For girls, the punishment for getting caught was slavery in the Federation as happened to one of our neighbors. For women, they offered slow execution as an example to others. One of the Federation's favorite sentences was the cage, submerged at high tide.

When I didn't move fast enough, Mom shook me. "No sulking. We need dry firewood. The skiff needs repairs. There's work to do. Get busy."

But I didn't want to lose another friend.

* * *

Colleen gathered anything that, if dry, would burn. She was a scurrying squirrel, afraid of being left behind like a neighbor up north. When they lost their fishing gear during a storm and couldn't gather enough food, they left their youngest daughter on a barren island for the bounty hunters.

Unburdened by knowledge of the past, surviving day-by-day was all that mattered to Colleen and our neighbors. The Federation had turned us into wild animals on the verge of extinction. *Not me.*

I was determined not only to survive, but to help neighbors be self-sufficient and independent of the Federation. Maybe someday, before the swamps disappeared altogether, we could make it over the Wall. Somehow all that ancient knowledge I'd gathered from illegal books had to figure in. But first, I needed my salvage partner.

Deep in the recesses of my gut I knew she needed help. Magdalena was an only child. Her mom often got depressed that their island was too small to survive on and that storms kept coming. With each passing day, my friend had to do more fishing, gardening, repairs, and cooking by herself. She had to take on her mom's role, and she was only fifteen.

While Mom made repairs inside the cabin and Colleen gathered wood on the other side of the island, I grabbed my log-boat and paddled out into the frothy channel. The current was strong, but heading my way, out toward the outer islands where Magdalena lived. My heart ached over what I might find.

My arms burned from holding Colleen during the storm and making repairs. I didn't want to defy Mom, who had provided me a home and sacrificed for schooling, but I had to know if my friend had survived.

I paddled hard across the channel and made my way around a nearby island. The Krause family was making sure scavengers knew they still claimed their island. Ms. Krause waved. I wasn't a scavenger risk with my small boat, so I waved back.

"Need any help?" I asked.

"We're fine. Watch for scavengers southeast of here. And bounty hunters."

"Thanks, ma'am."

Along the southeast side of Krause's island, I hid among cattails and sunken bushes. Thanks to binoculars and my memory, I confirmed that the bounty boat I'd seen before was the one now hovering in the distance. It had the same registration numbers on the bow. One bounty hunter stood at the bow using binoculars.

Next to her were two girls in chains. Their green-canvas clothes were tattered. Their faces looked more resigned than terrified. I recognized one from out Magdalena's way, a girl whose mom couldn't afford to barter for school. Maybe she would be better off in a Federation work camp, but even twenty-first century nations had abolished slavery.

Unable to think how to rescue the girls from armed bounty hunters, or how to feed them if I did, I headed north, paddling hard against the swift current dragging debris of people's lives. In a round-about way I made it to an island across from three scavenger boats. As I feared, they'd converged on Magdalena's home.

I didn't see her. I didn't see her cabin, either. Logs from her home scattered about the island and floated in the channel nearby. Two green-clad scavenger women dragged timbers toward the shore. A crew of three loaded the fresh-water tank onto their boat. Another carried the water purifiers. Two other scavenger boats waited in the channel for the first boats to get their fill and leave. Competition was fierce but they didn't want to lose their lives bickering over a rich find.

A gray Department of Antiquities boat motored past. They were the police, the authorities, but the agents made no attempt to stop the scavengers from stripping the island and Magdalena's family of what they needed to survive. They also didn't interfere with the nearby bounty hunters, since they delivered girls to be slaves.

With the current in my favor, I set out toward the side of Magdalena's island away from the scavengers. The bubbly channel was strong, shoving my log-boat out toward the open sea, a mile away. Despite aching muscles, I paddled hard across the current to reach quiet eddies on the southeast side of the island. Trees had uprooted from a storm surge. Bushes had pulled free. Logs floated in the water, banging against my boat. I pulled closer for a better look.

Magdalena huddled in a pool of water amidst rocks, her head bobbing. She didn't seem to notice me. I recognized the paralyzing storm tremors. When they caught hold, the mind shut down.

I paddled beside her. "Where's your mom?" I whispered.

Sweat made it hard to tell, but I gathered she'd been crying until her tears stopped. She pointed across the channel.

"She left?" I held her feverish hand, which trembled in mine.

Magdalena shrugged. "House gone. Water gone. Mom gone."

"Is she coming back?"

Eyes vacant, my friend shook her head.

"We have to claim your island."

Her words came out slowly. "I can't make it. Mom took the boat."

"Did she go for help?" I said as encouragement.

Magdalena looked up, her eyes those of an old woman. "Mom said wait for bounty hunters. They'll come after scavengers leave."

"No, Magdalena. Don't. You don't want slavery."

9

"No boat; no water; no home. I'm a burden with no hope."

"Stop it. You're my friend. We'll work this out. If you won't defend your home, then climb in."

She shook her head. "No use."

"Hurry," I said. "A bounty woman is coming." I pointed uphill.

A woman in a brown alligator outfit with binoculars scanned the small island. She spotted us and hiked down the slope toward us.

Upon seeing the bounty hunter, Magdalena climbed in.

"Wait right there," the bounty woman said. She lifted a tranquilizer gun but lost her footing.

I placed my crossbow in my lap. I was tempted to shoot, but while Antiquities agents wouldn't stop bounty hunters and scavengers, they would hunt me down for shooting one.

Before the alligator woman raised her gun again, I paddled around bushes and cattails, staying out of the swift current until we were halfway back to the scavenger cove. The bounty hunter followed us partway but then hurried to the cove, where she'd left her boat.

"Paddle," I said to Magdalena. "The current is too strong to do this alone."

We pushed out into the main channel. Immediately the rush of water shoved us toward the sea. Branches and clothes rushed our way, threatening to entangle us. I aimed into the current to lower our profile and we paddled hard toward a nearby island. When I looked back the bounty hunter boat moved away from the cove.

We paddled around the island, keeping to quieter waters and then pushed against the current to reach another island. We hid in the cattails, thankful for the smallness of my log-boat. Magdalena trembled, drawing into herself like a wounded mouse.

After the bounty boat passed, we crossed another channel and another. By the time we reached the Krause family island, the bounty boat had turned around and was scouring nearby islands more closely. We barely made it into the cattails before the boat began motoring around Krause Island. It was too late to try for my home island. Besides, I didn't want Mom turning Magdalena over to save Colleen and me.

Bounty hunter pay was high enough for them to keep hunting until they found us, and to make trouble for Mom if they didn't. With nowhere else to run, we climbed out of the log-boat and carried it up behind rocks.

From where we crouched, we watched the bounty boat with three green-clad girls chained to the bow railing. Two brown-clothed bounty hunters scanned us with binoculars. I hoped in the oppressive heat that they couldn't pick up our infrared signals. I pulled out my crossbow in case. I wouldn't go without a fight.

"Wouldn't it be better to let them take me?" Magdalena said. "I don't want to be a burden."

"Don't you dare," I said, huddling next to her. "Friends look out for each other."

"Even my mom didn't stick around."

"That doesn't mean you have to give up."

I knew it was hard, but hard didn't mean you surrendered. Magdalena squeezed my hand in a manner that got me worried she was saying goodbye.

"If they catch you, they catch me," I said before she did something rash.

She sighed. "You're the best friend in the world. Do you really think I have a chance?"

I didn't, though I wasn't ready to quit. "Together we'll search for your mom and a place for you to live."

"She's not coming back."

"Why? What happened?"

* * *

Magdalena shrugged and watched the bounty hunters circle the island. She leaned closer and whispered. "The wind tore the door off the cellar. Mom had a ratty old doll from her mom. The wind took the doll. In the middle of the storm, Mom ran out to find it. I couldn't stop her from rowing away. A big wave destroyed the boat. I'm sure she drowned. All for a stupid doll." Despite the turmoil in her face, she shed no more tears.

I was in shock. I felt attachments to books I'd read, but I couldn't imagine going into a storm to protect them. Life was too precious, even in the swamps.

After the bounty boat circled the island the third time, it crossed to Mom's island. She stood on a ledge, her rifle pointed out. I couldn't hear what they said, but the bounty boat moved on. I aimed my bow in case they returned.

"We have no surplus," a woman's voice said from behind us.

I turned to face the barrel of Ms. Krause's shotgun.

"We're leaving, ma'am," I said. "Just avoiding bounty hunters."

Her face softened. "Sorry. I don't know which is worse, the storms or the scum who thrive on suffering."

"Thanks for your hospitality, ma'am." I dragged my boat toward the shore.

Magdalena helped me put the log-boat into the water. We checked one last time for the bounty boat and paddled against the current into Mom's cove.

Gun at her side, she greeted us by her skiff. "You abandoned your chores."

"I'm sorry, Mom. Magdalena needed help. She lost her mom and her home. Scavengers cleaned the place. Then bounty hunters came."

"So that's why they were here." Holding onto a tree trunk, Mom moved along a rocky ledge. Then she turned to Magdalena. "I'm very sorry for your loss. We don't have much and Regina should be helping to fix things."

"I'm sorry, ma'am," Magdalena said. "I should have let the bounty woman take me."

"No, Mom. We can't. She's my best friend. We have to help. At least until we find her a home."

Mom sighed. "You'll have to scrounge extra food. We lost fruit and fish are scarce."

"I understand, Mom."

"Do you?"

"I won't abandon my friend. We'll just have to salvage the depths."

"Antiquities patrols are making that impossible. They don't want us disturbing cultural artifacts they deny exist." Mom turned to Magdalena. "If you help make repairs, you can stay the night."

"Thanks, ma'am." Magdalena forced a smile. "How can I help?"

* * *

After Magdalena helped us tar the roof and walls, I led her down to my log-boat.

Colleen joined us. "Can I come?"

"Mom needs you to look after her," I said. Colleen wasn't buying it so I added, "We have little room for salvage as it is."

"Mom will make me do your chores."

"I'll make it up to you. We need to find something so Magdalena has a home."

Colleen sulked on the ledge above the cove. I disassembled my crossbow, wrapped it in plastic, and stored it in a compartment in the back of my boat. Then I dug up a corroded aluminum funnel with a sealed opening. I placed the funnel in the middle of the log and paddled away from shore.

"What do we need that for?" Despite the spark of curiosity, Magdalena's eyes drooped, showing the full weight of losing her mom and home.

I paddled us out into the channel, and let the current carry us east. "The funnel is great for catching rain water."

She drew her arms in tight to her chest: storm tremors.

"No more storms today," I said, feeling terrible for scaring her. I was asking too much to ask her to dive after losing her mom and home, but I needed help. Besides, we were doing this for her.

Tears streamed down her cheeks. "I don't know what would have happened to me if you hadn't come."

"That's what friends do," I said, paddling us northward.

She shrugged. "I know you want to help, but do we have to dive?"

"We find the best salvage after a storm stirs up sediment. Maybe it exposed something we can barter."

I wanted to rip the resignation from Magdalena before it got both of us killed. This wasn't her first loss. She and her mom had been unable to save her sister five years ago during another storm. It was hard not to resign when each year the seas swallowed more of your life. Becoming a Federation slave sounded reassuring, except I'd heard rumors of girls dying in the mines and factories and being worked to death on the farms.

We approached the waters over what had been a Richmond suburb. Scavengers had picked islands out here clean of human habitation and trees. Denuded islands offered no resistance to storms or sea. Only swamp grasses thrived.

We headed across a wider channel between smaller islands. A bounty boat motored across the horizon. I saw in Magdalena's eyes a yearning to be taken care of, a desire for shelter with food.

I pulled into the cover of cattails. "That's no life for you," I whispered as if the bounty hunter could hear this far.

"I don't want your mom mad at you and ..."

"She won't abandon me on account of you."

Magdalena picked up her paddle. "I won't let them catch you."

I was thankful she'd found something to keep her from giving up. I glanced at the cloudless sky. The sun blazed down on us like a fire—well it was.

While we waited for the bounty boat to pass, a gray Antiquities boat rounded a nearby island. Two girls stood chained to the bow rail. I recognized them from the school Magdalena and I went to. Antiquities agents scanned our island with binoculars and motored off. If it hadn't been for my spotting the bounty boat, the Antiquities agents might have caught us. I couldn't leave Colleen like that.

After the Antiquities boat was gone, we circled the barren island to make sure no one else was there. Then we headed across water above a satellite community outside of Richmond.

We reached a small, treeless island. Waves broke in the distance where the sea fought the river current. Fishing was good out here though scavengers could grab you. One time I'd dangled my catch below the boat to keep it from scavengers, but hungry predators ate my fish. There was nothing more discouraging than getting home to find you had nothing left.

We hid the log-boat amidst cattails. Then I pulled four breathing bladders from a compartment of my boat. They weren't as good as scuba tanks, but those were luxuries reserved for bounty hunters and Antiquities patrols. "Are you up for this?"

Magdalena nodded though her heart wasn't into it.

"Do this for me," I said, filling my breathing bladders. "I don't want to lose my only friend."

She laughed until tears streamed down her cheeks. "You're the only friend who came to check on me."

"Then it's settled. We do this for each other." I clasped her arm. "Blood sisters."

Magdalena nodded with enthusiasm and made sure Colleen's breathing bladders were full.

I attached mine to a belt holding up my canvas shorts, removed my green canvas top, and slid into the water. Then I pulled goggles over my eyes. I checked the knife on my belt and ducked under water to make sure there were no gators or other predators lurking nearby.

When I surfaced, Magdalena was ready to dive. She managed a smile. "Thanks. I won't let you down."

The sun in the western sky cast no shadows onto this side of the island. I pointed westward. "The dive site is a thousand feet out and straight down. Don't use breathing bladders until we dive. It's a hundred feet down. Don't take any chances." I didn't remind her of the bends. I didn't need to give her something else to worry about. Besides, if it came to that, the bends would be the least of her troubles.

* * *

When we reached the spot I picked to dive, I double-checked the position of the sun and the island.

"This is it," I said.

"Let's do it," Magdalena said without conviction.

We attached breathing bladders and descended into the cloudy depths. Sediment was shifting in the strong channel current, making it as dark as the storm at night.

I held off using my only flashlight so we didn't trigger Antiquities sensors. Magdalena swam close, bumping into me to get her bearings. Before we touched bottom, I turned on the light for a quick look.

Below was an Antiquities mine in the shape of a crab. It hadn't been there during my last visit, which meant they'd found this spot and were interested.

Magdalena pointed to the mine and then up. I pointed across a plateau toward a stone house I'd visited once before. The roof and shingles were gone, probably wood frame and fiberglass, judging by scraps I'd found. The doors and windows were gone. Yet the walls stood guard like a medieval castle, resisting the ravages of time— I'd read too many history texts.

I took a good look, turned out the light, and swam closer.

From my last visit, I knew the drywall had turned to mush. The wood furniture had rotted, though varnish remained as a ghost of what lay beneath. Metal cabinets and appliances had corroded to uselessness. I'd salvaged the stainless cook-wear and bartered for a goat to provide my sister milk. She owed her good bones and teeth to that goat.

The homeowners had been well off, with nice things even by twenty-first century references. They'd been frugal, using solar panels that lay corroded and in pieces behind the house. A wind generator had collapsed nearby. I'd hoped to salvage something off it, but from the look of nearby debris, someone had already stripped the site. I also expected to find something of use in the home's basement, which I hadn't had time to explore before.

On my prior visit, I'd cursed how these well-meaning souls had protected their precious books and electronics in biodegradable plastic. Maybe they didn't know. The paper had turned to mush, the memory devices had given up their memories, and the electronics had corroded beyond repair.

How did I know they'd used biodegradable plastics? Sometimes the plastic seams or seals survived, looking similar to their less biodegradable cousins. These folk had been good for the ecology but bad at preservation. The only surviving evidence that they had books—a title on leather with no book pages behind—was volume one of Lamella Marshall's *History of the Twenty-first Century*.

As Magdalena and I approached the house, I flipped on the light.

Since my last visit, Antiquities had strung wire across all the openings on the first and second floor. There would be sensors if we got any closer and trip wires intended to cause injury or warn us away. Beyond the deterrent, Antiquities had made no attempt to preserve anything. Why would they? The only past they preserved began with the Federation.

I swam up over the house and studied the shell of the structure. Wires, various shapes of mines, and traps covered the open roof gap like a spider's web. There was no going in. If we survived whatever blasts they might trigger, we would be out of oxygen long before Antiquities patrols came for us. The site had been worth a look, but we would have to scrounge harder for a way to help my friend.

Motioning for Magdalena to follow, I turned off the light and swam toward the island. I recalled texts mentioning how cautious people had become before the Federation. This stone house overlooked a now sunken valley a hundred feet below. There could be more sites down there, but they were too deep to dive with breathing bladders. Only Antiquities agents and a few bounty hunters had deep salvage tanks.

In the shimmer of light from the surface above, something caught my eye. It wouldn't have been visible from the stone house even before the deluge. Yet it held possibilities, if for no other reason than it was higher than the house, a safe haven from earlier floods.

As I swam closer, a cave opening appeared. Magdalena tugged

my arm to swim uphill to the island. I shook my head. Then she pulled me toward the cave.

Under water, you had to trust your partner, so I followed her into the cave before looking back. Three points of light moved in the distance. Antiquities divers with tanks.

If Antiquities caught us out here, they would use starvation, torture, and submerged cages until we told everything we knew about underwater treasures. Or so I'd heard. No one ever returned from interrogation. If they were lucky, or unlucky, they became Federation slaves.

The outside lights moved toward the stone building below us. When they were gone, I flashed my light to take in as wide an image of the cave as I could like a camera. In the ensuing darkness, Magdalena squeezed my arm. I sensed her terror, but forced myself to concentrate on the image I'd seen, committing it to memory. The cave was shallow, natural as in not made by humans. It might have provided short-term shelter from past storms until it flooded. I imagined a campfire, though evidence would have washed away long ago. Aside from providing shelter from Antiquities agents, this was disheartening. There was no salvage potential.

Magdalena brought my hand to her breathing bladder; she was worried. She pulled me toward the cave opening to leave. Outside, the three lights moved closer. In the muddy water I could just make out the gray wetsuits worn by Antiquities divers. I couldn't let them catch my friend and give her the worst slave job they could think of. Environmental-hazard cleanup came to mind.

I pulled her deeper into the cave. We couldn't risk my light to hunt for another way out. Instead, I stood where I'd gotten my image, closed my eyes, and studied it again. There were no breaks in the wall before me. My hands and foot found no openings behind. Then I looked up at my remembered picture.

Barely visible at the top of the frame was an opening, a possible tunnel that would have been useless when this was dry. The ceiling above the cave and into the tunnel were black, charred blacker than the rest of the cave. Either that or it was a darker shade of rock.

I switched breathing bladders, directed Magdalena's hands to do the same, and swam up to the opening in the ceiling. It was just big enough for us to swim through if we tucked the breathing bladder around our necks. I tugged Magdalena up, let her feel the gap, and entered into darkness that let me realize how much Antiquities light was entering the cave. By feel I made my way up, horizontal, and up some more, haunted by the nagging fear that this was a dead-end or worse, a trap.

The tunnel curved and grew narrower until I could barely squeeze through. Then it widened. Unable to feel the depth of space around me, I flipped on the flashlight. Magdalena swam up behind and glanced around in amazement. We were in a chamber, a room carved by human hands. There was a path from where we entered to a full sized door. Lining the walls around us were plastic shelves holding stacks of plastic packages, and not the biodegradable variety.

Magdalena pointed to her breathing bladder and to the space we'd left. I shook my head and gave her the Antiquities signal. *What if they're following us?* After all, they had much better diving equipment.

We needed to keep moving, but I was drawn to a richer discovery than any I'd uncovered so far, one that could secure a home for my friend.

Nearby was the six volume set from Lamella Marshall, well preserved. I held the volumes with reverence, unwilling to let Antiquities destroy these as they had so many others. There had to be hundreds or thousands of physical print books. My breath caught.

There were too many books and they weighted too much to carry with us. Besides, we were running out of oxygen and we didn't know how to reach the surface.

Nearby was an old Franklin stove, protected in plastic. Magdalena pointed to a stack of pots, dishes, silver, and home-building tools. That was what we needed. But books nourished the soul. *Well, not if we didn't survive.*

There was no way back: we didn't have enough oxygen and Antiquities agents were waiting. We had to find a way forward and a way to stop agents from following. We dragged the Franklin stove to the tunnel leading down, pushed the top into the hole, and shoved it down as far as we could. Then we wedged tools into gaps between the stove and the tunnel walls to slow them down.

I pocketed a plastic-wrapped memory chip I hoped held some of the written treasures. Maybe a well-preserved computer device that I'd rebuilt would reveal its secrets. I tried the door at the other end of the watery room. It refused to budge.

Magdalena's face took on the cast of storm terrors. I had to act before she panicked. Recalling twenty-first century how-to texts, I examined the door. The hinges were on our side. Using screwdrivers and pliers from among the tools, we removed the hinge post and pulled the door open.

Beyond was another flooded room with stairs that led up. Though there was no human dwelling on the surface, up was our best option.

We carried pans, silverware, and tools in their plastic containers into the next room and up the stairs. I figured we'd descended a hundred-twenty feet and risen eighty. We were close, though you could drown in an inch of water.

The stairs led past rooms with beds and shreds of clothes that had not survived the flood. If this had been the owner's shelter during the early years, I hoped they'd made it to higher ground. As we swam and walked up, I looked for exits. Then we hit a dead-end. The framed drywall ceiling had disintegrated, leaving stone above us.

Magdalena was gulping air, ready to panic. She offered me what she had left. I refused. I'd gotten her into this. I couldn't live with her death.

The owners would have needed a way to get fresh air and to exhaust cooking fumes from the kitchen below us. I led Magdalena above the kitchen to a large-diameter pipe. We used metal cutters, pliers, and a screwdriver to pry the aluminum open. Then we climbed into the enclosure. I turned out the light and followed the path up.

After ten feet, I tumbled out into the channel. Lights moved below us: a submarine, one of Antiquities' small drone-probes. Above was daylight. I helped Magdalena out of the tunnel and pushed her toward the island.

Tugging our treasure behind us, we kicked our way up the side of the underwater hill to the surface. We came up among cattails and sucked in fresh air. Magdalena was gasping. I pushed her to shore and dragged our treasure onto the rocks.

"That was close," she said.

I nodded. "You okay?"

She took a long breath and leaned back to take in the sky. She looked more alive than at any time since I'd found her. Trembling, she hugged me. The terror of what had almost happened seeped into my thoughts. We weren't out of this yet.

A gray Antiquities boat remained in the channel between us and home. Leaving our salvage on shore, we swam to the log-boat. I armed my crossbow and peered out through the cattails. Using binoculars I spotted the captain with a handheld device.

The sun would set soon, giving us the cover of night, but with temperatures dropping, our infrared images would show up on their scanners.

While we waited, we returned with the log-boat to our treasure and nibbled on cattails for nourishment. Then we fastened our salvage goods to the funnel and that to a hook beneath the log-boat. The funnel tip would reduce drag while we paddled up the channel.

Magdalena refilled the breathing bladders. "What if they catch us?"

"We dump the goods, dive, and hide."

She looked dubious but forced a smile.

As the sun set, the captain and a sailor changed into diving gear. They took extra scuba tanks and descended using a mini-sub to pull them to the depths. I didn't see anyone else on the patrol boat. They must have dropped off any girls they'd captured.

"We have to chance it," I said.

I handed her a paddle and aimed us across the swift flow of the channel, diagonally past the Antiquities boat. Struggling against the current would leave us exposed for a long time. Then I had a better idea.

We pulled up behind the patrol boat, where they kept a motorized dingy and tied our mooring rope. Magdalena looked ready to strangle me as I unlatched the tiny craft and attached it to the log-boat. After releasing the rope, we paddled away from the patrol.

When we were far enough out of earshot, I started the motor and used the dingy to pull us upstream. After we reached the channel north of my home, we cast the dingy adrift and paddled into Mom's cove. As much as we could have used the speed-boat, it had tracking chips.

* * *

As night settled in, Mom greeted us by her skiff. In the moonlight, Colleen stood on the ledge above scanning the horizon with binoculars.

"You had me worried sick," Mom said.

"We found something," I said.

"It doesn't matter if you don't live to enjoy it." Mom moved closer. "Show me your find."

Magdalena and I dragged the funnel and attached bundle from beneath my boat and handed items up to Mom.

She stacked them on a rocky ledge, helped us out, and gave us both a hug. "You did well. This will buy a good start for your friend. But you can't keep taking risks. I thought bounty hunters or Antiquities had grabbed you."

"They almost did, Mom. But Magdalena helped by watching my back. She's a great partner."

Magdalena looked puzzled. Then she squeezed my hand. "Friends watch out for each other."

I squeezed back.

Colleen clung to my other arm and stared up at me. A touch of her night terrors crossed her face and faded away. I kissed her forehead.

In the weeks that followed, rumors floated through the Richmond Swamps. Antiquities agents were hopping mad. Responding to tripped sensors around a forbidden site, two of their divers pursued a couple salvagers. Convinced they'd cornered the scoundrels, the divers removed their tanks to enter a narrow tunnel. A Franklin stove blocked their way. They ran out of oxygen before they could back out of the tunnel to reach their tanks and before a rescue crew could help them.

The treasure room might still be there when I returned. But in the meantime, Magdalena could stay with us until we found her a new home.

■ ■ ■

UNINTENDED REBEL

(Prequel to Rebel series)

I studied the black-haired Chinese boy on the roof of Michael's School for Boys. The private concrete institution stood diagonally across the street from my public high school with bars on the windows, razor wire all around, and security patrols dressed in black mechanical exoskeletons despite the heat.

"How did you end up behind barbed wire?" I whispered, wishing my words could reach him. "By the way, I'm Annabelle Scott, a junior. My mom's a state senator, in the political opposition; and I could get prison just for watching you." Yet I couldn't pull away.

I'd been observing the orange-uniformed boy for weeks, trying to get up the courage to do something. But what? I jumped like a paranoid squirrel at the slightest noise: the wind brushing against nearby solar panels. Or was that one of the wind generators shifting direction?

"Why does our glorious Federal Union lock you boys away?" A rhetorical question I was forbidden to ask. "Are you a dangerous brute as my Cabbage-faced Civics teacher says? Would you hurt me given a chance?"

Another white flash came from his direction.

"Are you signaling me?"

I wanted to talk with this "other" to find out if we had anything in common. I couldn't use e-com; our beloved Federal Union tracked every wave. They probably had eyes watching me even then. Separating the boy from me was a busy street filled with bicycles and buses. Next to the boy's institution and directly across from me was the local hospital, a building that looked the mirror image of Michael's so-called school.

While viewing the Chinese boy's cute masculine face through my wide-spectrum monocular, I'd puzzled for weeks on how best to communicate. He looked my way. My face burned. I crouched lower and adjusted my uncomfortable bra beneath my dreadful, school-approved bleached blouse. After weeks of wanting him to notice me, I now tried to act invisible. After all, I'd never seen a boy from closer than this.

What the heck. I flipped on a portable flash generator I'd discovered while checking out caves by the river and tuned it to an ultraviolet frequency. The dark-haired boy and I had been playing at something for weeks now. "Where are you from?" I whispered. "What happened to your parents? Do you read?"

Most boys didn't I'd been told. "Do you like sports, music?" Not that Union censors allowed much to choose from. I had to settle for playing a game of shadows and light with a boy I'd only seen from across the street and behind thick coils of concertina wire.

I flicked my beam three times and waited.

In the rising heat of the afternoon sun, the tacky tar on my school's roof began to ooze. I rose a bit, so it wouldn't stick to my regulation navy blue skorts. In the street below, a parade of electric buses shot past the hospital and scattered a cluster of commuting bicyclists.

A lone mechanized cop enclosed in dull-black shielding paced the exterior of the boy's school. My classmates were too paranoid or indifferent to talk about it. My mom swore me never to speak of it.

The mech cop checked the side of the building, glanced along the street, and ambled toward the other corner. I'd watched the hulking mechanical beasts outrun a bus to catch perps, mostly escaped boys. This one appeared bored walking the institute's perimeter. Up on the roof the Chinese boy acted as if he had all the time in the world. After all, he couldn't leave.

For months I'd watched Michael's School from this roof and from the office of Harmony Director Hanna Surroc, my Cabbage-faced Civics teacher. In all that time, I'd never seen any boys come out. They only went in. Every day the Union scooped up more boys from hiding places all over Knoxville and brought them to school-institutions like this.

A forest green armored bus parked out front to deliver another hapless soul. It tugged at my heart to watch, yet I forced myself to bear witness. Where did they put all the boys?

A violet light flashed from across the way. Then two more. *Not bad.* He got my message and responded one notch down on the light spectrum. *Now what?*

There was much I want to know: how he got there, what it was like inside, what he dreamed of. I tuned my beam and send three flashes of green. Sweat trickled down my neck and not from the steamy heat that beat down on another cloudless day. The tar felt gooey under my knees.

I spotted three faint yellow flashes from the boy's roof, hard to see without my monocular. I returned three faded orange bursts and waited.

Our school buzzer sounded. I was late for Surroc's Civics class. It would be the third time this month, and never for a better reason than I was sick of lectures about the Second Civil War and how great things have been since. I was due for more detention time. Harmony Director Surroc was convinced she could "reform" and "conform" me.

Can't wait!

On the curb before the boy's school, a tall redhead with a scruffy beard emerged from the bus. They'd bound his hands tight behind him. His muscles bulged. He wore a maroon tracking collar like my Chinese friend and chains around his ankles that forced him to take small steps toward the building. Like all the boys who arrived here, the redhead looked back before he entered the darkened glass doorway, a final glance at freedom. His sweet, frightened eyes called out to me. Then he was gone.

Looking up, I almost missed three red flashes from across the street. "Okay, let's see how clever you are." I tuned my beam to infrared and aimed three bursts to the Chinese boy. In the image through my monocular, he held something to his eye. I couldn't be sure if it was like mine.

Something rustled nearby.

I scooted behind one of the air conditioning units, hoping it wasn't Cabbage-faced Surroc or one of her snitches. I expected the Chinese boy to beam back red, asking for a message in the visible range. He surprised me with three infrared bursts. Now that we were both signaling beyond the capability of the unaided eye, what did I want to say, and would he understand?

I'd taught myself Morse code since I couldn't think of anything else he might know. When I'd researched the subject, I came across flag signals, but that was asking for serious trouble. *Hello*, I send.

U have company, he sent back. Short brown hair.

It took a moment for the content of his message to register.

Someone brushed my arm. "Belle, I knew I'd find you here." It was my adopted sister, Janine, a year younger. I was the adopted one, and she wasn't to know.

"Babe, you can't be late for class."

She grabbed my monocular and scanned buildings across the street: the hospital and the institute. "Surroc is looking for you."

I didn't see the boy and prayed Janine didn't, either.

The door to the roof squealed as someone threw it open. "I know you're up here," old Cabbage-face said.

I wanted to strangle Janine for putting herself at risk for me, again, but I couldn't. "Stay here. I'll distract her. Then get your fanny back to class."

"Don't do anything crazy," she said. She knew me too well.

I kissed her forehead and ran across the edge of the roof. Tacky tar grabbed at my flats.

Surroc scooted back toward the steel access door to block my escape. "There's nowhere to go."

Old Cabbage-face was so predictable. I sprinted in those miserable flats, praying the tar didn't tear off their flimsy soles. As I headed down one wing of the school, I glanced back to see Surroc in a panic to stop me from reaching the other door.

She wasn't quick enough, but the door was locked.

"Don't make me put a collar on you," Surroc said.

That sent shudders up my spine. Criminals, boys, and those who breached Tenn-tucky's harmony laws had to wear the stupid metal chokers. Aside from having tracking devices, police remotes could trigger the collars to zap you. It was risky to swim or even take a shower with one on.

"Stop before you ruin your chance to enter the cop intern program," Surroc yelled.

That would almost make running worthwhile, though the alternative could be worse: environmental cleanup.

Glancing back, I saw Janine's worried face. *Get moving.*

She disappeared into the stairwell while Cabbage-face focused on me. Now that I'd protected my baby sister, I considered what to do.

Surroc stood with her hands on her chubby hips.

You've got me.

* * *

I reached the end of the main-building's roof and the drop to the auditorium below. I jumped. Disappearing from Surroc's view, I landed on all fours on another tarred surface, thankfully in the shade. I ran to the edge of the auditorium, counted my blessings that there was no concertina wire, and glided down the auditorium's drainpipe.

After I reached concrete, I sprinted along the side of the auditorium. Adrenalin kicked in as in cross-country. A bus almost sideswiped me. I jumped back into a mob of sweaty bicyclists. *Sorry.*

They scattered and rang their squeaky bells.

Before the next bus came, I sprinted down a side-street. *Never look back,* my cross-country coach had taught me. Of course she also taught there were no winners or losers, only harmony.

Right.

Along the sidewalk, women dressed in bland harmony-approved pastels scattered out of my way and stared with in-bred suspicion. I must be a criminal to run, to be out-of-place in town when I should be in school. Several used wrist phones to call it in, tying up emergency lines.

I turned the corner and slowed to a fast walk, hoping to blend in. Not likely with my school-approved pale blouse and blue skorts. I smiled at all the wary faces, nodded, and said hello.

Until I first became interested in the black-haired boy with almond eyes, I never thought how strange this might seem to our ancestors. I didn't see a single male on the streets, on bicycles, or in buses. Never had. While mention of such in school got you detention or worse, Mom often talked to me about life before the Federal Union defeated Outland rebels and chose to make the Union all-female.

How did they do this? Union mech warriors overwhelmed the

rebels, crushing them within weeks. Some said it was the hand of God, or Goddess, depending on your beliefs. Oh, you meant the fertility bit. Labs used EggFusion to fuse eggs from two women to create new life. You couldn't get pregnant unless you wanted to. Even then, you had to wait years for Federal approval for up to two daughters, and hope the process worked.

My thoughts returned to the Chinese boy with his charming smile. Well, one time I'd seen him smile. Most times he carried a focused scowl. I wouldn't smile either if they cooped me up in prison. Instead, I was stuck in an all-girls school with Cabbage-faced Surroc and her harmony rules. My joy came from watching her squirm.

There was something about connecting with a forbidden boy that appealed to me. Anything outlawed by our dear Union: energetic music, movies without harmony morals, and books Mom kept in her private library that could get her arrested. I liked anything that didn't smack of enforced harmony with officials telling me what I was allowed to do, think, and feel. Because if I did, thought, or felt something of my own, I was not being harmonious.

Bull.

Legs pumping, I turned another corner and almost tripped when roof-tar on my flimsy flats stuck to the sidewalk like tacky tape. I passed dozens more cams that could trace my movements.

Yeah, I'm acting stupid. At least I'm free.

I imagined myself as the Chinese boy escaping from the school-prison, breaking for freedom. I got this from the look on Red's face before they sucked him inside the institution. Maybe boys weren't that different from me.

The next street swarmed with large black insects: women cops in tarnished-black mechanical exoskeletons that gave them bus-speed mobility and brute force to contain any threat, even the most brutish of men. I'd never seen any except on security vids the school fed Janine and me to entice us to sign up for security careers.

Not on your life.

I turned and sprinted away from the boy's school. I expected old Cabbage-face to pop out at each street crossing. She wasn't fast enough, but that didn't help. I was running in circles, postponing the inevitable.

Breathe. Savor the moment.

In the past, Surroc would have caught me already. Some said I was pushing for attention or testing our security. They were wrong. Though I hated school, I loved to learn.

When she'd caught me before, old Cabbage-face made me sit in her office, where I could watch the prison-school. When I didn't show the proper humility, she put me in solitary for an hour: the broom closet. There I was alone with my thoughts.

The swarm of mech cops meant someone had escaped from Michael's. Was it my Chinese friend, the redhead in shackles, or someone else I might have seen? This excited my blood to keep running.

If I were a boy, I'd cross the river into forested hills. But the river was too wide to swim and Union mech patrols monitored every bridge. There might be a safe-house nearby, a traitor who harbored boys. But who would risk helping an escaped boy given the penalty of prison or worse?

My eyes searched for clues of the boys. I was excited and terrified, the result of too many harmony tales of the dangers boys presented. As I ran, women kept their distance. Bicyclists crossed to the other side of the street. Doors closed to Federal Clothiers, Federal Hardware, and Tenn-tucky Bistro, with shopkeepers no doubt forewarned by e-cast to be on the lookout for boys or for me. Surely I wasn't that important.

While in great shape, my legs rebelled from tension, and not having clear goals. I turned the next corner, past a Union Burgers & Subs. A boy with dark hair tore off down an alley before I could see if it was my Chinese friend. I was impressed he made it this far and felt propelled to chase after him.

One of the huge black insects cut me off and sprinted after the boy. No doubt the cop inside radioed my location. I doubled back and reached the next corner, Tenn-tucky Clothiers. Three more mech cops entered the street. Cams and cops surrounded me.

My e-com vibrated. I ducked into a Union Burgers & Subs to catch my breath. Two mech cops sprinted by. My e-com flashed: Surroc. That meant she was back in her office to look up my number. *Focus on me, not Janine, you fat cabbage-head.*

I squirted myself a cup of water and ducked into the restroom. It was a lousy hiding place. I hoped they didn't have cams. The thought gave me the creeps. Too many voyeurs got their kicks watching us common folk. I knew it was a stretch to think of myself as ordinary when my adoptive Mom was a state senator. Yet she was an outcast herself, in the dreaded opposition, nothing to be envied.

When my e-com vibrated again, I almost turned it off. It was Mom so I picked up.

"What in the world?" she began and fell silent.

Guilt enveloped me. Another stupid prank. More black marks on my permanent record. My entire future disintegrated before me. I didn't have the heart to tell her our precious Janine almost got caught. Even that was my fault.

"I'm sorry, Mom. I hate school and all the ..." I wanted to say lies, but caught myself. The Union monitored all frequencies. I didn't need them questioning Mom. She was already in enough hot-water with the governor and Tenn-tucky's Police Chief.

"Get back to school," Mom said. "Take whatever punishment they give with grace."

"Yes, ma'am."

"Don't sass me."

"No, ma'am." *Please don't un-adopt me.*

* * *

I headed out to what had become deserted streets. People hid when mech cops appeared.

Seeing a black-demon mech cop run down the street got me wondering if the boy was still free.

Hugging the storefront of Federal Office Supply, I inched my way back toward school. I was in no hurry either to run into mech cops or to face Surroc. Halfway down the block, I spotted non-mech uniformed cops surrounding Michael's School. I backed into an alley to conceal myself and wait for my opportunity to cross.

Someone grabbed my wrists. "Got you, you little street urchin."

I wrenched free before she could tag me, and moved toward the street. Cops lined the sidewalk. No escape. I turned and studied my cop's face: weathered, tough, no nonsense, not a lump of buttered cabbage like Surroc. The cop held a taser, aimed, and fired.

Awaiting the jolt, I froze. Muscles twitched in anticipation of paralysis to come. I fell back against a stone wall and braced myself. The worst part was losing control and peeing your pants, the ultimate humiliation. I whimpered, hating myself for acting so weak. She had me; yet she didn't trigger the juice.

I hung my head and acted submissive to let her know I wouldn't resist. Surroc was one thing. Cop-trouble was far worse, particularly since becoming a cop was the best I could hope for, according to my Harmony Director. In any case, I didn't want to add assaulting a cop to my list of offenses. "Please, I'll return to school. Promise."

I looked behind the tough cop to see her partner, a big-boned brunette. She adjusted the maroon collar on the boy I'd seen earlier. It wasn't my Chinese friend or Red. This one was smaller, round eyes, sandy blonde hair, and looked ready to pee himself if he hadn't already.

If he's dangerous, I'm a giraffe.

The big-boned cop pushed the boy toward the street, his arms cuffed behind him. She even chained his legs so he couldn't run. Like he could get far with that collar. Cops would have had him in convulsions before he got ten feet.

"Take him in," the tough cop said. "I'll handle this one."

* * *

While the big cop led the boy out of sight, I hung my head and leaned against the stone wall. "I know truancy is a serious offence. I won't do this again. Seeing that boy scared sense into me," I wanted to help the boy. He reminded me of protecting Janine.

"You're not half as scared of the boy as you should be," the cop said. She removed the taser contacts from my neck. "You've been shocked before."

"Yes, ma'am." Twice, which was one reason I didn't run. Getting shocked while running could lead to serious injuries.

"Annabelle Scott, isn't it?" The cop checked her wrist-com. "I'm Lieutenant Brooks. You're mother is a state senator."

I nodded. My blood was ready to boil. I hated people bringing up Mom, as if my sins had anything to do with her. I turned to run. The cop hadn't reloaded her taser. She'd have to outrun me or use her regular gun.

Before I could make my move, she slammed me against the wall of the retail store. "You're full of piss, aren't you?"

I'd never heard an adult use such language. My face burned. Her fist stung against my shoulder. She had power I hadn't anticipated from someone not wearing a mech suit.

"I'm a nobody who skipped school," I said, eyeing the street for an escape.

31

"I doubt that." She stepped back to reload the taser. "Someone signaled the boy's school. I suspect you. I always get to the facts, so don't bullshit me."

"No, ma'am." I was used to predictable Surroc, not this. "I want to return to school."

"What's your hurry? I'm not done with you."

Feeling trapped got me thinking about jail: torn from Mom and Janine. Plus all the shame I'd bring to my family for breaching harmony. My eyes filled with sissy tears.

"You romanticize being some modern-day Juliette, don't you? This isn't a game."

Really? Seems like one. Who is Juliette?

"Someone helped these boys escape. If I find it's you, I'll send you away for a long time."

I couldn't see how I'd helped anyone, except by distracting the cops. She'd said boys, plural, though. Did the Chinese boy make it? What about Red?

Scanning the narrow alleyway, my mind flooded with ideas: distract cops, give boys directions. What else could I do? Then I imagined Janine, tearing herself apart because she couldn't prevent me doing something stupid.

"Why would I help boys when they're all brutes?" I asked to keep Brooks busy.

"Spare me your class regurgitations. You think you're one tough chick, don't you?"

A pathetic one right now.

She studied her wrist-com, and then looked at me. "I see you're security-tracked, which means you know better. I should haul your ass to jail. Your mom might get you out in a week or so, but that would cost her. I don't think you want that."

"Please. I promise to be good."

"You don't get it. Helping boys is a federal offense, serious jail time."

I stared into her tough face. I was quaking inside. Then I reached a moment of clarity. "You have other plans for me, don't you?"

Brooks grinned. "I believe you have what it takes to be a cop if you lose that chip on your shoulder."

"So you're offering me jail or become a cop?"

"Cop internship, actually. It would focus your energy. I'd be willing to sponsor you in the hope of turning you around. Two afternoons a week at first. Then we'll see."

"What about child labor laws? At fifteen, shouldn't I be out having fun, instead of working my butt off?"

Brooks narrowed her eyes. "State deems you're old enough for the intern program. I should think that's preferable to the alternative."

"There you are." A plump cop with captain stripes approached. Captain Barb Voss looked bigger in person than in our school security vids. "Lieutenant Scarlatti said I'd find you here. Ah, you caught our little troublemaker."

I held my tongue and mulled over Brooks' offer. I didn't want to become a cop, enforcing rules over what people could say and do, and imprisoning boys. However, helping boys was a serious offense. As a minor I might get two weeks, maybe a month. Then I'd be out and no longer tied down with expectations of cop internship. Unfortunately, being security tracked meant that my future was limited. Cop was my best option.

The captain sneered at me. "Why expect better from the daughter than from her obnoxious mother? You're all trash. I've got a jail cell for you."

Brooks pushed me aside before I could defend my family. "Captain, I'd like to bring this grunt into the intern program. She's security-tracked. Why waste a valuable resource?"

Voss was another reason not to become an intern. I'd have to deal with her hatred for Mom, which was all over the news.

The captain glared at me, then at Brooks. "You sure you want to put your entire career on the line for this trash?"

"Let's not judge her based on her mom. I think we can turn this one around."

I stepped back into the alley's shadows wishing I could become invisible. I didn't want jail. I needed Janine around to quell this anger before I did something even more stupid.

While Brooks argued with Voss I heard my sister in my head, where she'd taken root years ago. After all, she was the smart one, studying a year ahead of her grade to challenge me to pass my classes. She would say, "Internship provides job security," as if I cared, "and gets us out of school two afternoons a week."

Most important, I didn't want Janine to follow my example. She would. I was such a bad influence on her. I couldn't hurt Mom and by association put a black mark on Janine's record. I looked at Brooks and Voss arguing. I'd never had anyone except Mom stand up for me before and Brooks knew nothing about me.

"She's a lost cause," Captain Voss said, reminding me of Surroc. *I'm not a lost cause. I'll prove it.*

My gut screamed to say no to the cop internship. But once I did jail time, they'd watch me more closely and tag me with a parole collar for all to see. However stifled I felt already would get much worse. On the other hand, I could take up Brooks' challenge and find a way to stick it to Voss.

"I'd be honored to take the challenge of becoming a good cop intern," I said.

Voss stopped and squinted at me, as if she could zap me with her mind.

Inwardly, I smiled. After all, if I became a cop intern, Surroc wouldn't be able to inflict her little punishments on me.

Brooks shook my hand. "You won't regret it."

We'll see. I smiled.

Voss screwed up that cow-face of hers and glared as if she could stab my eyeballs. I'd welcome that to escape her spiteful image.

"One step out of line and I'll nail you and your entire family," she said. "Don't think I won't."

I didn't for a moment doubt she'd try. I held my facial muscles taut as a statue to deny her any reaction. It was something I'd had considerable practice with at school.

Captain Voss spit on the sidewalk, something that would have gotten me arrested for disharmony. Then she strutted away with her look of disgust.

I focused on the retreating cow, swishing her tail with her awkward waddle. Brooks slapped a wrist-com like hers onto my left wrist. I pulled away, but she held firm.

"This links you into our com-net so we can contact each other at any time."

"And so you can track my movements," I added. It almost felt like that boy's maroon collar.

Brooks nodded. "If you get into trouble, all you have to do is push these two contacts." She pointed to opposite sides of the wrist-com. "That brings help."

Just what I needed, a way to have cops on my backside.

"Don't trigger this accidently or as a prank. You don't want to know what hell can descend on you."

I had a good imagination, enhanced by prior close encounters of the wrong kind.

"Shall I report to the cop station tomorrow?" I asked in the hope of getting away before things got worse.

The deserted street came back to life as cops faded away.

"You start now," Brooks said. "One of the boys still eludes us. We believe someone helped him. Heaven can't help if that was you, but I'm offering you a way to redeem yourself."

Stunned, I stared at Brooks; then lowered my eyes. "Why me?"

"We picked up your signal. You may not have helped the Chinese boy escape, but you were in contact with him."

I closed my eyes. *Dumb. Dumb. Dumb!*

My breath caught. He could still be free.

Brooks' eyes narrowed, studying me. My marble façade crumbled. I was betraying myself, but I recovered. "Okay, so I've seen boys across from my school. If the Union doesn't want me seeing them, why locate them so close. Why not send them to the country?"

"You're a clever girl. You tell me."

Not used to this type of interrogation, I hesitated. "They couldn't find a better use for a closed mental hospital?"

Brooks nodded. "Sounds about right. Help me find him. In return, I'll sponsor you into the intern program. That'll keep your sorry ass out of jail, for your benefit and for your family."

She had me on a very short leash. Not seeing any alternative, I nodded. "What do you want me to do?"

"Follow me." Brooks led the way back toward school. "As an intern, you need to learn to follow orders. Can you do that?"

Do I look like someone who follows orders? "Yes, ma'am."

She studied me and kept moving. "Anything you think of that might help me catch the boy you're to tell me. Is that understood?"

"Yes, ma'am." I struggled to keep up with her cop boots. My tacky flats kept sticking to concrete like chewing gum. "Why don't we track his collar?"

"Now, why didn't I think of that? He masked the transmitter."

Clever. I tried not to show my reaction, though I got the impression Brooks could see through me. "I don't see how I can help."

Brooks grinned. "Because, you little urchin, you play hide and seek with your school, and with cops. Think. Where would you go?"

Scanning stores, restaurants, and Union-run apartment buildings, I considered where I'd go to escape ever-present cams and infrared sensors. But I didn't want her catching my friend. "Isn't an intern supposed to get some kind of brainwashing?"

"It's called indoctrination. For now, we'll keep this simple. You're not to act on your own. You'll shadow and watch me. You'll advise me with any thoughts no matter how bizarre that might lead to this boy."

A snitch in other words. I felt as if I were betraying my own sister. "Do I get a weapon to protect against this brute?"

"No, so stay close."

I noticed how respectful pedestrians were when Brooks passed, nodding and smiling. It made me wonder whether they had secret thoughts that they hid behind their facial masks.

We reached my school with the auditorium to my right and administrative offices to the left. "I don't think a boy would come here." At least I hoped not. Having them near Janine gave me chills.

Harmony Director Surroc greeted us on the front steps, beaming. "Thanks for returning our runaway, officer. Sorry for whatever trouble she caused." Her bright-white teeth grinned with delight. I could almost see the slow churn of her brain thinking up new punishments for me.

Standing on the bottom step, I adopted a zoned-out face. After all, if I was going to be a dumb blonde, might as well look the part.

Brooks met old Cabbage-face halfway and shook her hand. "Afraid we have police business. We need her help."

Surroc looked stunned, which stretched a grin onto my face. Cop internship might be tolerable if it got old Cabbage-face twisted in knots.

"I don't understand," Surroc said. "She skipped school. Truancy is—"

"Annabelle is helping with an investigation as a test for entry into the intern program."

"Oh? She hasn't ... I mean she's been ... we can't allow this."

"Need I remind you that police business takes precedence over school matters?"

"No," Surroc muttered. "But she's incapable of following rules. She'll make a poor cop." That sounded strange coming from someone who dangled cop as the carrot to get me to behave.

"I take full responsibility," Brooks said. "Thanks for your cooperation." She nudged me to follow her.

After we crossed the street, she stopped me. "We have our work cut out if you're to become a cop."

"Yes, ma'am, but Surroc—"

"Is a pompous ass. Still, you have to get past that if you're to survive in this world. You'll run into others like her."

"You mean Captain Voss?" I said.

"I didn't say that."

"Then you agree."

Brooks pushed me against a Tenn-tucky Electronics storefront. "Don't mess with me. Don't mistake my offer as weakness."

Rubbing my sore shoulder, I wanted to hate Brooks for being one of the thugs hunting down my friend, but she was a puzzle. I felt like an alien plopped into some foreign world where all the rules had changed. I'd learned to deal with old Cabbage-face. Brooks seemed one step ahead of me.

All I knew was I didn't want to go to jail. "Now what?"

* * *

Brooks checked her wrist-com and frowned. "Think, Annabelle. If you were on the run, where would you go?"

Trap! Don't give up your hiding places.

My mind spun. *Can you read my thoughts? Am I that transparent?* It made me wonder if I'd been kidding myself that I've gotten away with white lies at home and dark ones with Surroc.

"As a girl, I'd find a friendly place; find someone to talk to. If I distracted her long enough, she might agree to help before she became suspicious and turned me in."

"For this exercise you're a boy."

"I've never considered it from their perspective." *A lie.*

"Look, I know you're only here as an alternative to jail. This is important. Think of the implications if this boy gets away."

He could find his family and have a life.

"You don't seem convinced," Brooks said, nudging me along. "If he gets away, he could help rebels. He could assault girls at your school, even your sister."

Janine!

I couldn't breathe. I didn't want to believe that's what he wanted.

I calmed myself as I did when old Cabbage-face interrogated me. If I were an imprisoned boy, I'd want freedom, not to go around hurting people.

"What if he's not a brute?" I asked. "What if he just misses his family? Surely you don't believe taking his family away is right?" I shut up before I said too much, before Brooks arrested me for disharmony.

She hesitated. "That's a decision for the Judicial Board, young lady. Our job is to stop boys running around with their collars masked so we can't find them."

"If he walked down Main Street in an orange outfit, with his neck puffy to hide his tracking collar on a steamy day like this, don't you think people would report him?"

"Where were you when I got this assignment?" Brooks frowned. "Of course he's not walking the streets like that. He must have had help to mask the device and change clothes."

"Who would help him?"

"Underground Railroad," she said.

"That's a myth." I'd read about this group during the first Civil War, though the Federal Union denied its existence today. It would imply there were boys who needed saving.

"It's not a myth. Let's start with the institute." Brooks headed toward Michael's School. "Assume you're inside the school and you want out. How do you go?" She glared at me as if I would know. After all, I'd just escaped my school.

"I'd have to see inside the school to figure that out."

"Okay, but no tricks."

"Are you kidding? We're going inside?" My throat closed. Brooks kept surprising me. Or she was trying to trick me.

While picking up her pace, Brooks sent a message on her wrist-com.

Avoiding a few bicyclers, we crossed the street in front of the hospital and turned toward the school. On the other side of the street, old Cabbage-face stood on the steps of my school. I almost felt sorry for her. Brooks had removed her daily joy. I grinned.

"How can the boy mask the collar's tracking device?" I asked.

Brooks stopped. "Are you messing with me?"

"No, ma'am. If I'm to help, I need to know what he does."

She nodded, though I saw doubt. "Aluminum seems to block the signal." She resumed walking.

"Aluminum foil? It can't be that simple." I studied the large windows of the hospital and the barred ones of the boys' school next door for any hint of my friend.

"Double-wrapped, yes."

"What about infrared? Can't the school scan buildings and count people?"

"Their scanners can't confirm male," Brooks said.

"He found a way to mask infrared?"

"Remind me not to underestimate you."

I felt as if I'd given away one of my secrets.

"There are ways," Brooks said, "but quite complicated."

"Nano-fabrics?"

"Polymer blends. It would require help on the outside."

I wanted more details, though not at the risk of turning Brooks against me. Aluminum foil I'd remember. It might help mask my student ID and travel fob.

As we headed toward the boys' school, three black-shielded mech cops circled the grounds. I would have loved to see their puzzled faces. All this technology to catch a single boy and he was winning. Got to love him for that.

Regular uniformed cops mulled around outside the large concrete hospital to my left. No way would I want to be stuck in there. An ambulance pulled up the drive. Someone could have helped the boy that way. I kept that to myself.

As we passed the hospital, I stared down the narrow alley that separated it from the school. I spotted hundreds of cams and sensor boxes covering the area. The boy would be crazy to cross there.

Brooks studied me. "I see wheels turning. Spill. Tell me what you're seeing and thinking."

"If he crossed this alley, you'd have him in custody."

"And?"

Or he'd be in the hospital, where I wouldn't go. Too many people and cams. "There are no windows or doors on this side of the school."

"You're not convinced."

"What are your cams telling you?"

Brooks continued toward the institute entrance. "Cams tracked three boys down this alley. We caught all three."

"And the boy you found."

Brooks frowned. "He left out the back. We've caught all four who showed up on cams. The Chinese boy you were watching never did."

"So he's still in the school."

We reached the Michael's School entrance, the one I'd watched earlier from the roof of my school. The windows were black. A grandmotherly woman wearing an administrator's suit like Surroc greeted us with a scowl. She moved with more determination than I first expected. "We've searched the entire school. Everything's in lockdown. You won't find him here."

"We'd like to look around," Brooks said while shaking the woman's hand.

I wanted to ask how the administrator knew for sure that he wasn't in the building. I held my tongue as she led us inside what felt like a dungeon. The entryway was dark except for light from the street until the blackened doors closed, robbing us of the last flicker of daylight. A blast of cold air caused me to shiver after the sticky outside heat.

Someone was watching. I felt violated in the dark with sensors picking up more than my infrared signature: probably chemicals, heart rate, and a full body scan. After a few moments, another set of doors opened. Lobby lights bathed us. An officious woman sat behind a metallic desk. She studied an array of screens, no doubt reading scan tests on me or watching hundreds of cams and sensors from all around the school.

If this hadn't been my idea, I would have turned back. "Any way he could have jumped off the roof and bypassed cams?"

The administrator studied me. She looked much younger than I'd thought, though she would benefit from a more colorful wardrobe. "Overlapping cams cover every inch of the grounds. Infrared sensors aimed in and out would have picked up any signature as it did for the four boys you've caught."

I was surprised she talked so openly in front of me. Adults other than Mom rarely did. The administrator must have assumed I was already an intern. Brooks nodded for me to continue.

"When did you lose their collar signals?"

"Before they crawled under the wall."

"A tunnel?"

"A gap they enlarged. We've since sealed it. We've examined every inch of the school perimeter and closed off similar escape risks."

I was enjoying this challenge. Thinking of escapes connected me to stories of my father escaping when I was three, though they caught and executed him. Keeping Brooks and the school administrator busy might help my friend.

"What about jumping off the roof?" I asked.

"A parachute we would have detected."

I was stumped and impressed. "No closet he could be hiding in?"

The woman shook her head.

I was torn between figuring out the puzzle so I could meet the boy, and not wanting him caught. I wandered toward huge steel doors on the hospital side of the school. Security was tight. I reminded myself that I'd never seen any boys coming out of this institution.

The unnamed administrator—she didn't offer and wasn't wearing a nametag—unlocked the doors. She led us down a high-ceiling concrete corridor with dingy beige walls, smelling of sweat and ammonia. I sneezed. Rows of steel doors lined the hallway.

"Are these classrooms?" I asked, going with the school-titled name of this place.

"Boys aren't like girls," the administrator said. "You have to keep them separated or they cause trouble. We've triple checked each room. There are no boys here and no possible escapes."

She didn't offer to show me inside. This time Brooks glared at me not to push it. I sulked down a corridor that resembled a dark medieval dungeon, the jail cell that cow-faced Voss had for me. These were so unlike my classrooms it made me wonder what I'd been griping about. Surroc was a declawed pussy cat by comparison.

My stomach did somersaults. I stifled a sneeze. It made no sense to come here if we couldn't ask questions and inspect these rooms. I already knew the answer. The Chinese boy didn't escape this way and there were things the administrator didn't want me to see: torture chambers, beatings, bloody experiments. I tried to shut off my imagination.

Brooks shook me. We were back in the lobby. The tour was over. I was relieved and disturbed.

"Do you have a basement?" I asked.

The administrator scowled. This time Brooks stared at the woman.

"That's how the boys escaped," the administrator admitted. "They found crumbled concrete and dug their way out. This is why we keep boys isolated."

"Can we see?" I asked.

"More of what you've seen, only underground."

"Humor us," Brooks said. She winked my way as the administrator led us toward elevators across the lobby.

I didn't want to be friends with Brooks. She was working me to get my guard down. But I didn't like the alternative. I imagined myself in this place with no windows and no escape. If Brooks brought me to scare me, it was working.

The woman took us down to the real dungeon. As soon as we got off the elevator, the dank odor made me sneeze and cough. I wouldn't be any good escaping from a place like this.

Lights were dim. The concrete floor carried dark stains. I told myself it was only my imagination. "What's the difference between these rooms and the ones upstairs?" I asked. Cam boxes poked out of the ceiling every ten feet."

"Those are classrooms and meeting rooms. These are for boys who misbehave."

"Any boys escape from …" I stopped before I said "cells."

"No boys escaped from solitary," the administrator said. "The walls are foot-thick steel and nano-polymer reinforced concrete. Even if a boy found a hammer and chisel, which they can't, it would take him longer than we hold him here to break out. We inspect these rooms daily. The four we caught escaped from a break in the tunnel in back using a sonic excavator someone smuggled in. We've reinforced that break and two others. We've also installed sensors to detect sonic equipment."

I wasn't convinced. "How many rooms do you have down here?"

"Sixty-four."

"How many are in use right now?"

"That isn't relevant," the woman said. "I already told you no one has escaped from solitary."

My heart tightened at the thought of so many boys in solitary, or even one, my friend. "I was hoping to see one."

"Lieutenant Brooks, is this necessary?"

"Let us see," Brooks said. "After all, you don't know how the other boy escaped."

The administrator took us to the end of a long yellowed corridor and unlocked a thick steel door. When she opened it, the smell was overpowering of feces and urine. I gagged yet forced myself to enter.

A yellowed light came on with dim illumination to confirm the horror. Straw covered the concrete floor that measured seven feet on a side with no sink or toilet. There was no sign of human waste, though the stench lingered. Along the hospital side, scratches marred the wall as if someone had tried to dig their way out of this hell-hole, a feeble attempt, probably with bloodied fingernails.

"You've checked all these rooms for any sign that someone dug their way out?" I asked. I held my breath and left the room.

"Thoroughly," the administrator said. "I told you it would be unpleasant. Boys are pigs. Good thing we've banned both."

Stepping across the corridor to escape the stench, I glimpsed a side hallway. "Does that lead to the hospital?"

"When we have emergencies, we prefer not to parade boys along the street. These doors are secure on both ends. I assure you the boy couldn't waltz out that way without a lot of help."

I smiled. The last place I'd want to land is a busy hospital. I didn't want to think how injured a boy would be before they'd move him.

I couldn't get out of Michael's Prison fast enough. When we reached steamy fresh air, I ran to the street and stopped at the sight of my school across the way.

Brooks held my arm to steady me. "You insisted. Now what aren't you telling me?"

I looked up. "How can we treat boys like that?"

She looked around. "Watch your tongue. Ears are everywhere."

"I don't care."

Brooks shoved me along the sidewalk. "One more word and I'll arrest you. Now, unless you want me to back out of our deal, tell me how the boy escaped."

Helping to capture my friend went against everything I believed in. The thought churned my stomach after seeing the conditions at

Michael's. I didn't want to betray him, but I couldn't survive jail, and it would kill Mom and Janine.

The massive hospital before us from the right angle could have been a cousin to the boys' school. Built around the same time, the institute had served as a mental ward before they turned it into Michael's School for Boys.

"The hospital. Of course." Brooks grabbed my arm and dragged me into the emergency room.

While she talked to a brunette at the nurse's station, I watched a mother and her two little girls. Tears filled my eyes for the brother I would never know, for what I was about to do to the Chinese boy to save myself. Yet, if he was in the hospital, what was he thinking? My only hope was to make this another distraction, another false lead buying him time. To salve my own conscience, I settled on that.

From the emergency room door I watched mech cops surround the hospital. Plain-clothed and uniformed cops entered in droves and fanned out. There must have been fifty, all for a lone boy who had to be petrified. I was.

"Come on," Brooks said. "Let's check out this side of the tunnel for clues."

I followed her down a series of bright-white corridors. I noted similarities to the prison next door, except the hospital had tiled floors, drop ceilings, and brilliant-white paint.

When we turned the corner away from the nano-med wing, a nurse behind the counter caught my eye: tall, muscular, with a handsome Chinese face. He looked cute even dressed like a girl. I smiled and kept moving. I wanted to stop and talk, but then Brooks would arrest us both.

Suddenly, my body turned prickly with hot needles. I was endangering not only myself, but my Mom, barely surviving as a political outsider, and my sister who would endure the worse of my actions. The school and all her friends would ostracize her for our association.

"Did you see something?" Brooks asked, looking around.

"This place is a mirror image of ..." I almost said prison, "... school next door."

Around the next corner was an elevator, in the dingiest part of the hospital. Garbage pickup was to the left with a large locked bin for medical waste disposal. I wondered why my Chinese friend hadn't gone out with the trash. But camera boxes lined the exit and around the elevator, inspecting everything that left. He might have tried this and then scurried looking for another way out. And I brought the cavalry.

I damned my cowardice, my need for self-preservation.

When we reached the basement, Brooks led me to the hospital side of the tunnel connecting with Michael's. The worn and cracked concrete surprised me. This was a well-used passage, either from the mental health days or from the boys. All I had were questions that Brooks wouldn't or couldn't answer.

"As you can see," Brooks said, "the door is locked on this side with sensors monitoring the area. The hospital administrator is checking cam-feeds."

It was only a matter of time before they caught him. "Maybe I was wrong."

"Assume someone helped him."

"Whoever helped could have driven him away. In which case, he's no longer here."

"With so many cams and sensors, his helper might only have gotten him this far. Then what?"

I didn't like this game, but I couldn't stop. "Once he got upstairs, he'd be by garbage pickup. If I were him, I'd leave with the garbage, get to a dump site out in the country without cams and sensors, and make a run for it."

Brooks nudged me back toward the elevator. "Clever. We'll check the trucks and dump sites. Wherever he went, he's no longer down here."

Inwardly I smiled, yet kept my face as still as marble. I didn't want to give up my Chinese friend.

Brooks returned me to the emergency entrance and went to talk to that cow-faced Captain Voss. I felt terrible for what my Chinese friend had been through and for my part in bringing cops to the hospital. I hated being unable to play this safer with Brooks watching so closely.

The boy had been clever, hiding in plain sight here at the hospital. He could have waited, changing roles until the cops went away and then made his break. But I brought more cops.

A hand grabbed my shoulder. "What are you doing here?" It was Mom, her weathered face tortured with wrinkles. "I told you to return to school. I've looked all over for you."

"I'm sorry."

"Enough nonsense. Get your fanny home right now. Are you trying to ruin your family?"

"No, Mom. Lieutenant Brooks—"

"More trouble? What am I to do with you?"

"Mom!"

"Later."

Behind Mom I saw Brooks with that tall nurse in his ridiculous outfit, much too small for him. The lieutenant had already cuffed the boy whose only real crime had been wanting freedom. She tugged off his bonnet, revealing shoulder-length coal-black hair. When she ripped aluminum foil from the maroon collar around his neck, he offered no resistance. With so many cops, there was no point.

My stomach churned. My mind whirred thinking of any alternative, but it was too late. The boy looked at me with doleful eyes, breaking my heart. He blinked; twitched. Then I realized it was Morse code:

Thnx. UR not like them.

I wished there was more I could do for him. Maybe as a cop intern I could.

■ ■ ■

SHE-DEVIL ROCKS
(Story inspired by Lord of the Flies)

The private plane hadn't arrived yet. Bradley Munsch fidgeted in the shadows. The rest of his ninth grade class eagerly waited outside the hangar for their ecology field trip to Catalina to begin.

Angry gray clouds poured in to blot out the afternoon sun. It started to rain, which seemed unusual for Los Angeles in June. Hoping it would be a quick sprinkle, Bradley moved closer to his backpack in the hangar to stay dry.

Waiting was the worst part. Each moment their flight delayed was another that Bradley needed to find ways to avoid Malcolm. Two years older than the other boys, Malcolm Montgomery was number one, the tallest boy in the class. God in his infinite humor had seen fit to make Bradley the smallest of thirteen boys though not small enough to escape Malcolm's notice. Making matters worse, Bradley didn't feel lucky as number thirteen. He was safe as long as Ms. Rose was around. Malcolm made sure their teacher never saw his evil twin.

Bradley had done everything he could to avoid this school-sponsored trip. He complained to his dad that his stomach ached, which was true. He had a terrible headache. He even faked an ankle sprain, but nothing worked.

"You've been like this since your mother died," his dad had said. "It's been six months. Stop acting like a wimp."

That ended their little chat. After his mom had died, Bradley's

47

dad had placed him in this school with other boys who had experienced loss. He felt no kinship with the other boys, but his regular public school had been no kinder.

Shielded from their teacher by other boys, Malcolm eyed Bradley alone in the hangar. Covering his eyes from the rain, Bradley hurried around the other boys toward Ms. Rose.

"Everyone under the canopy," she said. Ms. Rose was only slightly taller than Bradley, yet all the boys straightened up when she spoke.

While the others moved under the canopy near the hangar, Malcolm grabbed Danny, number twelve, the second smallest boy, and hammered his arm with a big fist. Danny protected his face with his other hand.

Though five inches shorter, Miguel Ventura stood up to Malcolm. "I'm warning you."

Miguel was the second tallest in the class and had an older brother who roughed him up. Bradley had no brothers or sisters. Instead, he had a father who had introduced him to his belt for sulking or any number of other faults. Bradley swallowed hard.

A small jet taxied toward the private airport office.

"Everyone line up," Ms. Rose said.

As always, they lined up according to height, with Malcolm and Miguel up front and Bradley in thirteenth place. Danny covered the welt on his arm with his hand and hid behind taller boys in front of him.

"Thank you for arranging this fieldtrip," Malcolm said. He flashed the teacher his toothy grin. "This is going to be educational." He flipped back his bushy black hair, revealing lengthening sideburns. A head taller than the rest of the class, he was the only one who could grow thick facial hair.

Smiling, Ms. Rose walked along their ranks to ensure they weren't misbehaving. "I need to check inside to make sure we're cleared to leave on account of the rain. Malcolm's in charge until I return."

Ms. Rose marched into the small airport office. Coach and social studies teacher Mack McDonald was inside talking to a blonde girl who might have been our age. Eyes red, she looked miserable. She flipped curls out of her eyes, jabbed her finger toward Coach, and then toward the class. Bradley couldn't hear what she was saying, but she seemed pretty upset. He hadn't seen her before, but there was something about her that—

Thwack.

Like a baseball bat across the head, the thump sent Bradley sprawling onto the wet concrete out in the rain. He scraped his arm and knee, and prayed this would get him out of the fieldtrip.

"Little Bradley got himself a girlfriend," Malcolm said.

Danny cringed and scooted into the hangar to hide. Miguel followed. The other boys gathered around, watching, thankful that Malcolm's attention wasn't on them.

Bradley could always tell the days that Malcolm's dad belted him or his parents fought. It didn't seem to matter which. On those days, Malcolm looked for trouble, as if that would balance things.

The big boy with the bushy sideburns stood with the sly grin he got while thinking up new ways to show he was number one. "No girl will ever look at you, Little Worm," he said. "That she-devil will turn you into mush. Got it? Leave her to men like me." Malcolm puffed up his chest and flexed his arms.

As long as he was talking, he wasn't hurting anyone. Yet.

"Get up, Little Worm. Maybe you'll get lucky and get stranded at sea with her. That's the only way she'll ever look at you."

"Yeah, Little Worm," Tony the Joker added. He was number five and our class clown.

"Are there really she-devils?" another asked. It sounded like Jon, number eight and the chubbiest boy in the class. He couldn't help it. Both his parents were big.

Malcolm went to smack Jon. Miguel stepped in and Malcolm moved back, holding up both hands as if surrendering. He dropped his arms, straightened up, and gave his toothy smile.

Coach McDonald hurried out from the airport office, his short hair matted by the rain. "What's going on here?"

Malcolm bowed and stepped back to let Coach through. "Bradley fell," he said in his sweet voice. "I think he needs medical attention."

Coach helped Bradley to his feet, examined the rain-soaked scrapes, and scooped him up in his arms. He carried the boy into the airport office. Bradley felt further humiliated.

The coach set the boy on a sofa and waved his arm toward someone Bradley couldn't see. "You want to tell me what happened?"

Bradley wanted to tell, but his stomach knotted. He didn't want to imagine what else Malcolm could think up.

The blonde girl he'd seen earlier appeared with bandages and ointment. She was slightly taller than Bradley with striking cheekbones. She was very pretty up close, though her eyes were red from crying. She smiled and moved out of sight. He wanted to ask her to return. But he was too nervous to think what to say.

"This doesn't look bad." Coach dabbed the knee with a cotton swab. "Did someone push you?"

"I don't think so," Bradley said, disappointed that his scrapes wouldn't excuse him.

"You can tell me." Coach squeezed ointment on a bandage and slapped it onto Bradley's knee. Then he moved to the boy's arm.

Bradley looked up at Coach McDonald, who had told the boys to call him Mack. He had a rugged look with a square jaw. He was a tough man who didn't belittle Bradley like his dad did or attack him as Malcolm did.

Mack didn't believe that Bradley's regular bruising came from his being clumsy, but he never saw the worst of them. Bradley's dad had been careful not to leave a mark on arms, legs, or face, and Bradley was careful not to let Coach see his bottom. That wasn't proper. Malcolm hadn't been so careful, but Bradley didn't want more.

Coach ran his fingers through the boy's hair. "You'll be fine. Don't let this spoil your trip. Let it go and move on." He started to help the boy up.

"I can walk."

Coach Mack put his arm over the boy's shoulder and led him outside. The others had escaped the rain and boarded along with their luggage.

When he reached the plane, Bradley looked back to see the girl wave and smile. Bradley waved, smiled back, wishing he'd gotten the nerve to say something to her.

* * *

Coach Mack and Bradley were the last two on the plane. There were a total of fifteen passenger seats, one on each side of the aisle, and a small toilet cabinet in the back. Coach went back to sit beside Ms. Rose. The only other seat was by the door. Bradley took it. Danny, who sat across the aisle, sank as low as he could in his seat.

Malcolm was sitting behind Danny. "Had to make us late," he whispered.

Bradley watched the co-pilot, a late-thirtyish blonde with bouncy curls like the girl in the office. She checked what looked like a weather map. All she had to do was look outside at the gray clouds and rain.

"That she-devil grab your tongue?" Malcolm said.

The co-pilot double-checked the door and stood before them. "We're cleared for takeoff. Is everyone buckled in?"

From the back of the plane, Coach flashed a thumbs up.

"Then we're off. It'll be bumpy; nothing to worry about. It's a very short flight." The co-pilot climbed into her seat and the plane taxied for takeoff.

"Are you giving me your evil eye?" Malcolm asked as the plane lifted into the rain.

Bradley scooted into the corner by the window.

Malcolm leaned forward to see him. "You can't hide. You got a thing for Coach Mack's daughter, don't you?"

Feeling his face burn red, about to explode, Bradley stared out the window. Charcoal clouds darkened by the minute. Lightning hit the wing. He jumped, reached for the door, and stopped at the last moment.

Coach Mack hurried up the aisle and leaned over Danny. "Why don't you go sit with Ms. Rose?"

Danny looked relieved to be away from Malcolm. He hurried back.

Coach took Bradley's hand. "You need to sit. This storm is nothing to worry about, just a little rain that blew in." He checked that Bradley's seatbelt was tight and sat across the aisle in Danny's vacated seat. He watched Bradley with concern.

At times like this Bradley cursed not being even smaller so he could disappear. He would never hear the end of looking at the girl or Coach treating him like a baby by scooping him up in his arms. Bradley bit back tears and stared out the window as the sky grew even darker. Day had turned to night. Bradley hated storms. They reminded him of welts on his bottom the last time he wimped out over a little lightning after his mom had died.

The plane bounced up and dropped. Bradley's stomach was in his throat. He felt ill. Coach held out a bag. "In case you get sick."

"I'm fine," Bradley said, though he felt as sick as he had when his dad made him eat moldy bread. His dad forgot to buy fresh bread when his mom went into the hospital, and was in a hurry to leave.

"If you need anything, holler," Coach said. He walked up to the cockpit and whispered to the co-pilot.

Malcolm scooted up to the seat Coach had left and glared at Bradley. "We're taking you to She-devil Island. You wet your pants yet?"

For the first time that Bradley could recall, Ms. Rose caught Malcolm's evil twin. "That's enough. Go sit in the back, in my seat."

Looking ready to defy her, Malcolm remained seated. He clenched his fists on the armrest. His eyes tightened. His evil twin fought for control. Then he put on a smile and stood up. "Whatever you say, Ms. Rose."

She sat across from Bradley in the seat Malcolm had just been in.

Malcolm headed back then returned. While blocking their teacher's view, he placed a heavy hand on Bradley's shoulder and squeezed. "I'm sorry, Ms. Rose. I don't know what came over me. It's the storm and flying and all."

"We'll talk later," Ms. Rose said. "Sit in the back and fasten your seatbelt."

Malcolm bowed, sticking his large rear end into Bradley's face. He let loose what smelled like rotten eggs. "I need to tell Coach Mack something urgent. Then I'll sit in the back of the plane like a good boy."

"Make it quick."

Malcolm shared his evil-twin face with Bradley and squeezed into the cockpit area by Coach Mack. Bradley stared outside at rain hammering the wing and the ocean below. He prayed for this to quickly end.

The plane bounced up, down, and then right. Bradley waited for the aircraft to level out and his nervous stomach to settle down. Instead the plane dived like he'd seen in dog-fight video games. Only this wasn't a game.

Something shifted, maybe their bags in cargo beneath them. Lights blinked out. Lightning flashed outside. The plane turned left then right, dove, and nosed up. When it did, Coach Mack flew down the aisle like a loose ball. A sickening crunch of metal, plastic, and bone came from the back of the plane where he landed. Groans followed. Ms. Rose got up and carefully walked back, holding tight to each seat.

Malcolm clung to an aluminum handle that had kept him from falling. With his sly grin, he looked ready to pounce on Bradley now that Ms. Rose had gone.

Gripping the armrests, the smaller boy stared outside. Through the rain, seas boiled not far beneath them. A wall of land appeared up ahead coming right toward them. It didn't seem real, as if he was watching a video game. He curled his feet up under him and gripped the armrests.

The plane nosed up and slapped down like a fly swatter, throwing Bradley forward until he thought his seatbelt would cut him in half. The plane flipped upward. Metal squealed, plastic snapped. Suddenly, the cockpit was at a ninety-degree angle to the cabin. Then it was gone.

At some point Malcolm had moved to the seat beside Bradley. He ducked his head down, drew his feet up, and clung to his seatbelt. Fear had replaced his sly grin. He cringed as Bradley did before getting a beating.

Bradley looked away and tucked his body into a tight fist, covering his face with his hands. The fuselage tumbled onto its back, sliding backwards and upside down. Bradley hung from his seat, the belt digging into his churning stomach.

Windows blew out. The plane skidded through shrubs. The cabin split apart, scattering seats and passengers like bowling pins. Bradley's seat fell loose, hit the top of the headrest, and landed on its back. The seat skidded to a stop on a sandy beach. His head had missed the ground because he was so short.

Metal and other seats scattered around him. Angry waves pounded rocks nearby.

His heart raced until he thought it would explode. Heavy rains soaked him. The storm made it dark as night.

Bradley unfastened his seatbelt and rolled out onto the sand. He threw up. His stomach threatened to rip apart from pressing against the seatbelt. He ached all over and wondered what he'd broken. His foot hurt as if he'd twisted it.

Up the hill where the cockpit had broken off, lightning struck. Something sparked. An explosion followed and then fire.

Shaking, he got to his feet to look around. His foot shot out pain, more like stubbing his toe than a sprain, though.

Nearby, crawling out from under his seat was Miguel, the only boy who dared to stand up to Malcolm. He made guttural groans, got to his feet, and limped in a circle. His right hand twitched. Screams and moans rang out all around.

Number four Seth's head lay at an awkward angle beneath his seat. Bradley pushed him onto his back. Seth's head flopped to the side as if he were asleep. His mouth gaped open. Bradley hurried away. He stumbled onto two more boys who weren't moving. Then he spotted Coach Mack, his arms and legs at odd angles, his head dented in. He lay still on the beach. Bradley held his hand over Coach's mouth and felt no breathing.

The plane's toilet had landed on number six, Tad. Bradley tried to push it away, but couldn't budge it. Holding his stomach, he looked for Ms. Rose.

* * *

In a daze, Bradley walked past Tony the Joker, who mumbled to himself as he tried to undo his seatbelt. Bradley helped Danny out of his and then checked on the others. Numbers nine and ten lay on the ground twisted beneath their seats. Their necks looked broken. Bradley's stomach tumbled like a clothes drier. Waves crashed to his right. He froze.

Ms. Rose lay on her back, her hair matted, and her head on a rock. Malcolm leaned over her, giving her mouth-to-mouth. She wasn't moving.

Barely able to see through the rain and darkness, Bradley walked up the beach. He wiped his eyes. If Ms. Rose was gone then Malcolm was in charge. Malcolm wanted him dead. He'd said so only last week. Malcolm later said he was only trying to get a reaction, but Bradley wasn't so sure.

Several boys joined Malcolm by Ms. Rose. They looked scared. Bradley wandered, raindrops filling his eyes. Miguel clutched his right elbow and tried to stretch. He looked to be in a lot of pain. He was Bradley's only hope if there were no adults.

"Any idea where we are?" Jake asked rubbing his shoulder. He was the third tallest in the class and a fast runner who usually avoided Malcolm's wrath by siding with the bigger boy.

Malcolm let go of Ms. Rose. Her head flopped onto the rock like a wet dishrag. He stood up and glared at Jake. "Do I look like a traffic cop?" He glanced around with a bewildered look on his face, as if he couldn't collect his thoughts. His hands trembled. He kept clenching and unclenching his fists.

"Coach and Ms. Rose didn't make it." Jake's voice sounded shaky. "Five boys are gone." He sounded ready to cry, which was so unlike him. He also limped, holding his right arm.

"Who put you in charge?" Malcolm looked around at the wreckage and then at Jake. He brushed his wet hair out of his eyes.

"I think we need a doctor," Jake said, massaging his arm.

Malcolm looked down at Ms. Rose by his feet. For a moment he acted stumped. Then he glanced at the boys gathering around him. "Ms. Rose put me in charge." He took a deep breath and puffed out his chest. "Well then, we'll call this island She-devil Rocks. That's where we are." He tried to grin but the mask turned into a grimace.

"Not so fast," Miguel said, shuffling over. "If Ms. Rose can't speak for herself, I don't accept you in charge. In fact, I think you did something to crash the plane."

"Really?" Malcolm stepped back. "We're lost at sea and you want to challenge me."

"Maybe we don't like you in charge." Miguel pulled out a pocket knife and opened the blade. He held the weapon in front of him. "Anyone think Malcolm in charge is a good idea?"

Jake gave them room. "Ms. Rose needs a doctor."

"She's dead," Malcolm said. "She said I was in charge. Her last words. That makes it sacred."

Nearby number five, Tony the Joker, wrapped cloth around his ankle. Bradley half expected him to jump up and say, "Surprise."

Number eight, Jon, kept holding his head as if it were too big for his body. His taller and thinner friend Rick, number seven, had difficulty standing. Danny stumbled around.

"Jake's right," Miguel said, favoring his right leg. He still gripped the knife. "I say we—"

Malcolm approached and held out his hand. "I say let's be partners, then. Let's shake on it."

Miguel stepped back to keep his distance. Stumbling, he swiped his knife at Malcolm and fought to steady himself. Malcolm caught him. Instead of letting go, he grabbed hold of Miguel's right wrist, twisted it, and rammed the knife up into Miguel's chest.

"You dare swing a knife at me," Malcolm yelled. "You dare!

You're not my damned mother. You hear me? And you're certainly not my bastard father."

He dropped Miguel to the ground. "See what you've done? See what you've made me do?"

Noticing Jake and the others eyeing the knife, Malcolm took the blade, wiped it off on Miguel's shirt, and placed it in his pocket. "We'll have no more of that." He straightened up and grinned.

Lightning flashed up toward where the cockpit landed. A lone figure stood on the hill above the beach, the last person Bradley would have expected: the blonde girl from the airport, the one who had brought bandages. He started toward her.

Looking like a shaggy dog with his hair matted over his sideburns, Malcolm blocked the way. "No one goes anywhere unless I say so. Everyone gather whatever we can use and bring it to me."

Bradley looked up at the hill. The girl was gone. He hadn't seen her on the plane, hadn't seen how she could have gotten on. His mind must have been playing tricks.

"We should build a fire," Jake said, "or make a sign on the beach. That's what people do."

Malcolm tripped Jake, sending him sprawling onto wet sand. "Ms. Rose put me in charge, not you. I'm number one."

Favoring his right arm, Jake crawled away but didn't get up. "We need to do something so they'll find us and bring a doctor."

Jake looked like he wanted to stand up to Malcolm, but after what happened to Miguel, Bradley doubted anyone would.

Malcolm stood over Jake. "It's too wet to make a fire, you dumb klutz. Besides, the only 'they' going to find us are the she-devils." Malcolm kicked sand at Jake. "You want she-devils gouging out your eyes?"

"Do they do that?" Danny asked.

Bradley wanted to smack number twelve for drawing Malcolm's attention their way. Instead, he moved toward the crashing waves and recalled the first time Malcolm had ranted about she-devils, after a social worker had visited the school. Malcolm had carried on for over a week, but only while Ms. Rose couldn't hear.

Malcolm faked a punch toward Danny, who dropped to the ground, covering his head.

"Anyone else think they should be in charge?" Malcolm asked.

Everyone froze. Bradley held his breath and lowered his profile, hoping Malcolm wouldn't notice him.

Jake stood up, limped, and seemed to be doing better. "We need to let the authorities know where we are so they can help."

Malcolm spun around and stepped back so he could keep the other boys in sight. "Is that what you want? This is a damned sight better adventure than what the school planned. Who needs a stupid old ecology trip when we have all the nature we need right here."

"Malcolm, people are injured," Jake said. He eyed Miguel and stepped back.

"Dead," Malcolm said. "Say it. We have dead people. We'll bury them at sea like pirates do."

Bradley shivered at the word "dead". All four of his grandparents were gone along with his mom. His dad had spared him their funerals, which meant Bradley never got the chance to say goodbye. Seeing Coach Mack, Ms. Rose, and now six boys who weren't moving, Bradley couldn't decide whether his dad had done him a favor. He didn't want to say goodbye to Coach Mack or Ms. Rose. He trembled at the image of what Malcolm had done to Miguel. He was glad it was too dark to see all the blood.

Unable to breathe, Bradley wiped tears from his eyes and moved farther away. He was thankful the rain and dark shielded his eyes. He didn't need to give Malcolm another reason to single him out.

Danny hadn't moved from his spot curled up on the beach, protecting his head.

"I say we build a bonfire and burn the bodies," Tony said. "Then we can catch she-devils and burn them." He swung his arms as if throwing bodies into a fire.

The class clown's attempt at humor was shallow, his voice shaky. Still, the words sent chills up Bradley's spine.

Malcolm walked up to Tony and glowered at him. Then he grinned. "That's what we'll do. We'll build a huge bonfire … in the pouring rain." He punched Tony's shoulder. "Any other bright ideas?"

Numbers seven and eight, Rick and Jon, moved up the hill to get away from Malcolm.

Malcolm threw a stone, hitting Jon's back. "How you planning to guard against she-devils? Your only chance is to stick together and do what I say. Ms. Rose put me in charge."

Bradley looked at their teacher lying in the sand. She still hadn't moved. Her head hung back, her mouth open, gathering rain. Her eyes stared up, vacant. Was this how his mom had looked after she'd died of lung cancer? His lunch threatened to come up.

He looked away.

"We need a boat or something," Jake said. "Head east and we'll find land."

Malcolm grabbed the smaller boy's shirt in his right fist. "We aren't going anywhere. Got it. No fires. No signs. No boats. We're on a nature adventure right here. You with me or against me?"

Jake grabbed hold of Malcolm's arm, but he was no match for the bigger boy. "We stick together, like you say. I just think—"

"Leave the thinking to me. Got it?"

Jake nodded.

"Say 'Yes, sir.' That's what real people do."

"Yes, sir."

"Okay," Malcolm said. "Jake, you can be my first lieutenant. Your job is to see the others pay attention and follow orders. Can you do that?"

"Yes, sir."

"Good boy." Malcolm clenched his left fist and moved the arm a little. He let his arm go slack and looked at the other boys. "Now, we need a sergeant-at-arms."

"We've got no arms," Tony said, "excepting the ones hanging from our shoulders."

Malcolm swaggered toward the clown and grinned. "You've got the right idea, so I'll name you my sergeant-at-arms."

"What do I get to do?"

"You get to beat on anyone who doesn't obey," Malcolm said.

The big boys, who stood toward the front of the line, were getting ready to gang up on the smaller ones. *Thanks, Ms. Rose.*

"First order is for each of you to gather everything we can use for our adventure and put it right here." Malcolm used his heel to dig a circle in the sand. "If anyone finds a flashlight, bring it to me."

Bradley glanced up the hill for a glimpse of the girl. She wasn't there. It had to be his imagination distracting him. He moved to a couple of suitcases scattered on the beach. The other boys staked claim to what they'd gathered.

Rick hid behind his friend, fiddling with something. His cell phone. *Of course.* Bradley reached into his pocket. He still had his.

"Hey, hey," Malcolm said. "None of that." He grabbed Rick's cell phone. "We don't get to use these until we've had our adventure and I say so. Lieutenant? Master-at-arms? Gather the cell phones and give them to me." He grabbed Jon's cell.

Jake held out his hand. Bradley considered running instead of giving up his phone. But his foot hurt and he couldn't outrun Jake anyhow. He handed it over. Danny gave his to Tony.

Malcolm dumped the phones into his rain-splashed circle in the sand. "This is a start. Collect phones from the dead people." Being careful with his left arm, he dropped down next to Ms. Rose. He fished around in her pockets and tossed her cell phone on the pile.

Bradley moved behind what was left of the plane's tail. Clothes and suitcases littered the beach out to the waves. He wished he could have kept his phone, though there was no one he wanted to call. His dad would tell him to man up, whatever that meant. His teacher and coach couldn't help. He shed tears for his mom, but she was gone.

"Are you hiding a cell phone?" Malcolm asked, standing over Danny. He reached into the smaller boy's pockets and pulled out Danny's contacts case. Malcolm examined the case as if it could magically turn into a phone. "You'll get this back after you check each body and bag for cell phones. Got it?" He pushed Danny toward Seth, who remained strapped under his seat.

Malcolm kicked the seat, sending it and Seth onto their sides. "There. Find his cell."

Shaking, Danny rummaged through the boy's pockets. Coming up empty, he shrugged and held out his hands.

Number one smacked the wrists. "You failed." He pulled Danny over to the circle filled with cell phones. "Look here. How many do we have?"

Jake tossed another phone onto the pile along with two flashlights. "Thirteen."

Malcolm stopped to do the math. He hadn't tossed his phone in, which meant there was one missing, the one Danny couldn't find. With rain pelting them, Bradley dug into one of the carry-on bags.

"Close enough," Malcolm said. He shoved Danny onto the pile of phones. "Smash them."

"How will anyone find—"

"I'll keep one phone. You destroy the rest." Malcolm picked up a phone and hit Danny across the side of the head.

While everyone else watched Danny curl up on the ground, Bradley found what he was looking for. Seth's jacket had landed under scattered clothes and crushed bags. The boy's cell phone was in the left pocket. Bradley took the phone, stuffed it in his pocket, and hid behind the plane's tail. He was shivering in the rain.

Malcolm picked up the phones one by one and hit exposed parts of Danny's body: head, arm, shoulder. Then he slapped Danny's head.

"Hey! Stop!" Danny yelled. "I can't see. My contact popped out."

Malcolm stood up, as if stunned by Danny's outburst. "That wouldn't have happened if you'd broken the cell phones as I asked. Now get busy."

Danny cowered. "Help me. Jake? Tony?"

Tony wiped his ever-present grin off is face and moved away. Jake looked like he wanted to help, but he took one look at Malcolm and crossed his arms. Miguel wasn't there to stop Malcolm this time. Bradley wanted to yell that together they could take Malcolm, but then what?

"Rick? Jon?" Danny asked.

Rick tried to hide behind Jon who moved back.

"Bradley, help me."

In a moment of madness, Bradley responded to Danny's plea and took one step forward. Twinges of pain shot out from his foot. He scrambled back to the safety of plane debris before Malcolm noticed. After all, the bully wasn't picking on him.

He told himself if the other boys hadn't been there he'd have stood up to Malcolm, but that was a lie. "Man up," his father loved to say, but he wasn't there.

Feeling the phone in his pocket, Bradley took it out. He needed to call for help, but who could he call? He didn't want another tongue-lashing from his father for being such a wimp that he couldn't take care of his own problems.

Not knowing who else to call, Bradley pocketed the phone and ran from the cover of plane debris into the bushes overlooking the beach.

"Leave me alone," Danny yelled. "You're crazy, all of you. No one will rescue us now."

"That's the point," Malcolm said. "Finish breaking the phones."

"Stop it." Danny pushed between Rick and Jon and ran up the beach.

"Lieutenant, sergeant-at-arms, bring him back," Malcolm yelled.

Danny scrambled up the hill. He slipped and pawed at the ground. The gang ran after him. No contest.

Bradley felt terrible, but he didn't dare stay. He could be next.

Danny screamed.

Bradley threw up. Then he ran along the shore away from the others.

* * *

Behind the cover of a large rock, Bradley caught his breath. Then he tilted his head back to take in rainwater to clear the taste in his mouth. The rains stopped. Clouds cast a twilight glow over the beach he'd left.

Danny's last words lingered. "I can't breathe."

Bradley's throat tightened, as if this was happening to him. He kept moving.

When Danny's groans stopped, Bradley almost felt relieved. They brought back memories of his mom's more muted moans in her last days, begging for it to end. But Bradley had felt Malcolm's anger before and didn't want to experience it again. He threw up, and couldn't get the taste out of his mouth.

Malcolm yelled, "Anyone else want to disobey me?"

Bradley snuck away, hoping this rocky island was big enough to find a hiding place. He reached a ridge with exposed rock and no cover to hide behind. He moved sideways around it. Behind him a light flashed, then three, heading his way.

"Come home, little Bradley," Malcolm said in the pretend-polite sing-song tone he used with Ms. Rose. "Come back before the she-devil gets you."

Stumbling, Bradley rolled down toward beach, banging his sore arm.

"Come out or you're dead," Malcolm bellowed, his voice sounding too close.

Bradley climbed up muddy rocks, banging his scraped knee. He stifled a yelp and kept going. When he reached the top of the ridge, he spotted the blonde girl again. Matted curls framed her sad face and sharp eyes. She beckoned for him to follow.

The lights following him split up. One headed along the beach. A second bobbed behind him. The third veered off to his left. He didn't want Danny's fate.

He climbed, following the girl, but he couldn't catch up with her. He cut his hands on rocks and stumbled. He landed on his bad knee again. Malcolm and his boys were gaining. Bradley got to his feet and ran.

Around a ridge, he spotted the girl, urging him to hurry. He lost his footing and rolled down into a ravine toward her. Thankfully, nothing new hurt. When he looked up, she was nearby and then disappeared behind rocks.

Bradley crawled across the muddy slope after her. He slipped and slid down a slippery incline. When he hit bottom, pain shot out from his foot. He stifled a scream. He was in a hole, looking up at the stormy sky.

The pit's floor was muddy and mucky, with whatever lived in the grimy depths. His first instinct was to climb out, but the hole was six feet deep and Malcolm was up there.

"Where'd our slimy Worm disappear to?" Malcolm yelled from above.

Bradley's pursuers could discover him by shining their lights down into the pit. Yet it wasn't just a pit. There was an opening, a shallow cave. Bradley squeezed inside. Lights flooded the pit. The girl's face lit up across from him, wild-eyed, mysterious, curls plastered against her cheeks. She hushed him.

"I don't see him," Jake said.

"Me either," Tony added.

The lights faded away. The pit went dark.

The girl had saved Bradley's life and he didn't even know her name. He crawled across the slippery pit to the opening where she'd crouched down. "Wait," he whispered.

Fearing Malcolm might overhear and grab him, Bradley crawled into a narrow tunnel that led away from the pit. The ground was slimy wet from the rain and black as his closet at home where he'd hid from his dad's rage, only to get another belting for hiding.

Bradley scraped his leg against the side of the tunnel and remembered the cell phone. He pulled it out, activated it, and could see the tunnel led upward. Holding the cell in his teeth, he crawled forward despite his fear of what waited for him. His fingers squished through the mud. The rotten odor caused his stomach to churn. He kept moving out of fear that Malcolm would find his footprints in the mud. Come morning they would be easy to spot.

The cell light went out. There was dim light up ahead. At first Bradley thought he'd gone in circles and was returning like a moth to Malcolm's flame. He couldn't risk lighting the phone again. Instead, he held his breath to listen and crept forward.

The crashing of waves against rocks grew louder. The light was coming through an opening that must have overlooked the sea. A shaft of light shone through an ivy-covered opening into a small cave. He crawled out of the tunnel into the cave.

Spooked by a nearby presence, Bradley crawled back toward the tunnel. He stopped, caught his breath, and saw the girl in the shadows with a finger to her lips. He sat across from her. Waves broke below them.

Like back at the airport, his mind went blank. So much crowded Bradley's overworked brain that paralysis seized him. He started shaking.

Her eyes caught his attention. They'd lost the sadness from back at the airport. Even in the shadows, their intensity unnerved him. Her hands moved in an intricate dance as if she and Bradley shared a secret language.

Not understanding, he shrugged.

She looked disgusted, as his dad did when Bradley didn't catch on quickly enough.

He whispered, "I don't—"

She motioned for him to stop and pointed toward the opening, where Malcolm might be. Then she poked her head outside. She pulled her head in, put her hand over her mouth, and stabbed her finger at Bradley as she had at Coach Mack at the airport. She pointed for Bradley to stay and then vanished into the tunnel.

He didn't like feeling alone, except this was better than being with his dad or Malcolm.

* * *

Bradley couldn't stop shaking. Were Ms. Rose, Coach Mack, and some of the boys really dead? Despite years of Bible study he still couldn't fathom what death meant. One moment you're here. The next you're gone, somewhere hopefully better. When she was alive, Ms. Rose stood between Malcolm and what he wanted to do to Bradley. Coach Mack had patched him up. Now they were gone, like Bradley's mom.

Soon, he felt antsy sitting in the cave by himself. He parted the ivy and peered outside, taking in the salty sea air. The sky brightened. Waves crashed over rocks some thirty feet below the cave opening. The heights made him dizzy.

The cliff wall rose another ten feet above the opening. He couldn't see how to climb up. Besides, what if Malcolm or one of the other boys was waiting for him? He slipped back into the cave. The girl had returned with two branches about his height. She took a dark rock from her jeans pocket and began shaving an end of one of the sticks, sharpening it.

"What ya doing?" was the best he could manage. He felt stupid, slow-witted, like Malcolm often said.

Eyes wide, she pointed the stick at him with one hand and covered her mouth with the other. She tossed one of her sticks his way along with a black stone that looked like flint. It felt sharp like the rocks outside that had cut his hands. Now Bradley wished he'd paid closer attention at summer camp.

The girl showed him how to hold the stick and use the sharp end of the flint to shave off layers of wood to bring the stick to a point.

He didn't see the benefit of making a spear. They needed a grownup to rescue them. Did she know about her dad, if Coach Mack was her dad? He assumed such from the way she talked to him at the airport and from what Malcolm had said. After all, why else was she at the airport?

"How?" he started to ask.

She signaled him to shut up. He was glad she hadn't pointed her spear at him again.

When he finished sharpening his stick, she held out her hand. He passed her the sharpened spear. She smiled, nodded, and tossed it back. Now that her hair was dry, it bounced up as curls.

Making the spear with her gave him a distraction, a sense of doing something, but it couldn't block what Malcolm had done to Danny and Miguel. Still, just having her near was reassuring.

"I said throw him over." Malcolm's voice sounded like thunder above them.

When the words penetrated Bradley's fog, he began trembling.

His companion acted frantic. Carrying her spear, she crept from the entry to the tunnel and back. Danny's baggy shirt fell outside the opening, beyond the ivy. What crashed against the rocks was much heavier. *That could have been me.*

"Now the other one," Malcolm said.

Bradley stared in disbelief as a blue uniform fell from above: a man, the pilot. The body hit the water below with a thud. Bradley gripped the spear. His stomach churned. Sweat streamed down his neck.

He had hoped somehow that the pilot and co-pilot could have survived, despite how mangled the cockpit became and the explosion. Without them, there were no more adults to stop the bully. Bradley couldn't believe Miguel was gone, though sometimes even Miguel picked on the smaller boys to avoid a fight with Malcolm.

Bradley steamed. "Man up," his father would say. "Bullies take advantage of you if you don't man up." That was his only advice, which was why Bradley never told his dad about Malcolm, and why he couldn't call him for help.

"Toss the radio," Malcolm yelled, "and anything that links to the outside world."

"No!" Jake said.

"You want to join the pilot and Danny?"

"Make sense, Malcolm. After our adventure we want to be found."

"Why? Either the black box and the radio go over or you do."

"Fine, you don't have to be such a ..."

Jake didn't finish his thought. Several electronic boxes tumbled past the cave opening.

"Good job, Lieutenant. Now let's find that grimy Little Worm."

* * *

Bradley clung to his spear as if it could give him strength and protect him.

"We need food and water," Jake said from outside, his voice trailing away from the cliff's edge.

"Where's little Bradley?" Malcolm asked. "Whoever brings me Little Worm wins points."

"Hey," Tony said. "Maybe we could catch fish with the Little Worm."

Bradley shivered. Malcolm was a monster. A killer. Bradley had thought long and hard about why Tony and Jake followed Malcolm instead of standing up to him. The only thing that made sense was that while Malcolm's attention was on the smaller boys, on Bradley, he wasn't bothering Tony or Jake. That gave Bradley no comfort.

As soon as the voices faded away, the girl crawled out the cave entrance. She grabbed hold of the ivy, attached the spear to her belt, and pulled herself up. Bradley watched her scale the cliff face to the top.

Fighting his height-terror, Bradley looked down. Two bodies lay slumped over the rocks, splashed by the waves. The pilot had landed face down, with his head in the water. His body looked mangled as if his legs had snapped either in the crash or when he landed on the rocks. Blood pooled around his head. Danny lay on his back, his head bashed in. Two other boys lay on the rocks below. Bradley couldn't tell who. His gut churned, ready to make him throw up again, except there couldn't be anything left in his stomach.

Beside the bodies were bits of cell phones, electronics, and boxes. A charred orange box looked as if someone had hammered it, breaking it in two, and then set it on fire. A wave crashed in and carried part of it out to sea.

Above, the girl tipped her head for Bradley to follow. Feeling the cell phone still in his pocket, he slipped back into the cave. In the corner, he pulled away some loose stones and buried the phone.

Despite his fear of heights, Bradley's fear of being alone won out. He crawled through the opening and clung to the ivy. The girl signaled him to move faster. He locked eyes with her. It gave him the strength to stand on the cave ledge. When he grabbed hold of the vine, his hands were five feet from the top. *You can do this,* he said to himself by way of encouragement. *Just don't look down.*

He pulled himself up a foot and froze. His father's words rang in his ears, which got him trembling.

He climbed another foot and another. *Malcolm, what if he returns?*

Bradley looked down toward the cave opening. Big mistake. He immediately felt dizzy. Closing his eyes, he climbed another foot. He grabbed hold of the rocks above him and pulled himself up until he could see over the top. Lights danced in the distance, down toward the beach with all the debris. His companion moved away from the cliff's edge, motioning for him to hurry.

He didn't know what to make of the girl who hadn't spoken a

word to him. She wasn't the she-devil Malcolm had talked about. She had, after all, saved Bradley's life. So far. Except when she'd shaken her spear at him, she looked too angelic to be a devil. Yet, those were the worst kind. They fooled you into betraying yourself, or so Malcolm had said. Bradley wondered if some other kind of she-devil was the cause of Malcolm's anger, maybe the social worker. But that wasn't his problem.

Realizing he couldn't stay on the cliff's edge, Bradley pulled himself up onto rocky ledge.

Grabbing hold of her spear, the girl darted across a clearing behind bushes. She motioned for Bradley to follow and hurried away from the cliff. He eyed the cliff's edge and their hidden cave below. Ignoring twinges of pain in his foot, he ran after her to a clearing made by the plane when it crashed. One of wings and its engine lay near the cockpit, charred. Thankfully, the rain had kept the fire from spreading.

Plane debris cluttered the path down to the beach where the boys had ended up. Light, filtered through thinning clouds, cast a ghostly glow to the plane's debris. What was left of the charred cockpit lay on its side.

The girl ran beyond the cockpit and crouched down. Staying low, Bradley joined her. He wished for an adult to protect them from Malcolm. The pilot was at the bottom of the cliff. It looked as if someone had taken a hammer to the cockpit and pulled out all the electronics from the shell. The dashboard was black with soot, maybe from the lightning strikes or the explosion.

The girl nodded for him to follow her away from the cockpit. Debris trails spread out like star bursts where pieces had flown through the shrubbery. She followed one, climbed over a rocky ledge, and crouched down where she could watch the beach.

Below her lay the co-pilot, her blonde hair matted against her thin face. Her blue uniform was soaked red. Bradley hadn't ever seen so much blood. His stomach threatened to rise up into his throat. She turned her head and looked up at him. "Can you find bandages, antibiotics?"

She was alive, and she was an adult. There was hope.

He looked for the girl but couldn't see her. "Where?"

"First aid kit. Beside pilot's seat."

She grabbed hold of Bradley's arm. "Don't tell the other boys."

"No, ma'am."

Bradley hurried to the cockpit watching for the girl and hoping the first aid kit had survived. All he found in the cockpit itself had turned black with soot. He didn't see anything worth saving, let alone bandages. Not wanting to disappoint the co-pilot, he checked the bushes nearby and found a crushed box with a small bottle of alcohol, bandages, and both antibiotic pills and ointment. He carried them back to her.

When he reached the co-pilot, she struggled to breathe. Was this how his mom had been before lung cancer took her? His eyes teared up at the memory.

"Tell me what to do," he said.

She dragged herself to sit up and held out her left arm. Bone stuck out. She needed a doctor.

"Pour some alcohol. Then put the ointment on the bandage and wrap it tight."

Hands shaking, he did as she asked, all the time feeling nauseated by all the blood. He taped the bandage. "Anything else?"

She gasped. "My left leg." With her good arm, she tugged at a tear in her pants, widening it to show him a gash.

He repeated what he'd done for her arm and was impressed she didn't cry out. He wanted to. It looked like she was in a lot of pain.

"Go before those boys catch you."

Go where, he wanted to ask.

"There he is," Malcolm yelled. "Grab the Little Worm."

Bradley got to his feet and half-ran half-limped the other way. Footsteps crashed all around him, his and the other boys. He couldn't see how many.

"Whoever brings me Little Worm gets rewarded," Malcolm yelled.

The co-pilot let out a scream that turned Bradley's blood to ice. He wanted to go back and help her. But he didn't stand a chance with Malcolm, Jake, and Tony chasing him. He kept running.

Off to his right he spotted the girl on a ledge. Fuming, she waved toward Jake as if to get his attention. Jake was running in her direction. She didn't flee, as if she wanted him to catch her.

Bradley didn't know what took hold of him. His heart pounding in his throat. Suddenly he felt energized, as if something had jolted him alive. He ran toward the girl. Doom was bearing down on him and he wasn't fleeing, wasn't trying to save himself. He couldn't let Jake hurt his new friend.

As Bradley moved into the open, Jake turned his way. "There you are, Little Worm." Jake parroted Malcolm and ran straight toward Bradley.

* * *

Bradley veered left and spotted Tony the Joker running right for him. Bradley couldn't outrun either boy. He definitely couldn't escape both. He ran as fast as he could to draw the boys away from the girl with no name.

When he looked back, he no longer saw the girl, but the boys were closing in. He jumped across to nearby rocks and slid into a ravine. Ignoring the pain radiating from his foot, he rolled to his feet. He no longer saw Jake. Instead, he heard the boy moan, gurgle something, and fall silent. With Tony not far behind, Bradley ran. The girl stood up ahead, waving for him to hurry. He made it to where she'd been standing and found the pit he'd fallen into earlier.

Bradley didn't see the Joker, though rustling came from Tony's direction. Bradley jumped into the pit, landing like a cat on all fours. His foot screamed out again. He tumbled onto his side and crawled into the slimy tunnel on his hands and knees. Ignoring the rotting smell, he scrambled through the mud. He slid out of the tunnel, into the cave, and almost out the entry, which led over the cliff and onto the rocks below. Bracing himself against a cave wall, he caught his breath.

The girl sat across from him, cradling her spear. Her face filled with more sadness than he thought a face could hold, more even than his mom's the last time he saw her before she went into the hospital.

Bradley hung his head. "I'm sorry. I tried to save her."

"It was mighty brave of you to stand up to that boy," she said, her first words. "Foolish, but brave."

"I'm Bradley."

"I know who you are. You can call me Monique. I suppose you've earned that."

"How did you get here, Monique?" He liked the sound of her name.

"We need to find water and food." She grabbed her spear, climbed out the entry, and up the ivy.

It seemed strange on an island surrounded by water to imagine dying of thirst, but salt water could make you sick. He poked his head out of the cave, looked down, and shook so much he almost fell. He clenched his fists until the nausea faded.

When he stuck he head out again and looked up, she was studying him, her head tilted to one side. Not wanting to disappoint her, he grabbed hold of the vines and pulled himself up, keeping his eyes on her instead of the rocks below. Before he reached the top of the cliff, she moved away. He climbed up over the cliff's rocky ledge and joined her in the bushes.

Now that the storm had passed, the sky brightened. But the eastern sky was dark. Soon twilight would close in around them like a blanket. The night might help them hide, but Malcolm had lights.

Bradley followed Monique through the bushes away from the cliff with the cockpit to their right.

"We should help the co-pilot," he said after they crossed the debris clearing.

She hurried on.

He was stunned that she didn't stop to check on maybe the only adult still alive. The crash had banged up the co-pilot pretty badly. He wanted to give her more help. Not seeing the co-pilot where he'd left her, he hurried to catch up with Monique. When they neared the bottom of the hill, she turned inland and led him into a small cleft not far from the pit he'd fallen into.

Water bubbled up out of the ground. She filled her hands, washed away the mud, and filled them again. Then she drank.

"Shouldn't we boil this?" he asked.

"Boiling requires a fire," Monique said. "That would attract those boys."

He did as she did. The water didn't carry an odor and had a mineral taste that wasn't bad. She took more and so did he.

"Is Coach your dad?" he asked.

"Drink and let's go." She took another handful of water and sneaked down toward the beach. She picked up a long stick and handed it to him. "You should have brought yours. You'll need it."

"Where did you hide on the plane?" he asked. "I'll bet you snuck into the luggage area."

"Don't be daft." Taking the black stone from her pocket, she carved the tip of his stick into a spear and handed it to him. "Hold the spear like this to defend yourself. It makes a better weapon to scare than if you have to use it, but it helps to be prepared."

"For what?" He already knew. His knees wobbled thinking about it.

Beneath the darkening sky, lights from the other side of the island cast a halo over the crown of the hill.

"Come on," Monique said, "evening is a good time to fish." She entered the water and washed mud off her clothes.

"But we can't see."

She splashed him. "Don't tell me you're afraid of a little water."

While he washed off the mud, he felt exposed, out in the open. "You couldn't have hidden in the restroom. You were in the office when I boarded. And the restroom landed on the beach."

"Are you going to yammer or catch dinner?" She speared a fish and held it up. "See?"

"That was amazing."

"You do it. Imagine where the fish will go, not where it is."

"I can't see," he said.

She glared at him. He speared the water several times, hitting nothing but rock and sand. She nailed another fish. He pointed to lights heading their way along the beach to their left. She led him the other way, up the hill to the cliff. When they reached the top, she stopped in a clearing overlooking the sea and showed him how to use her gray stone to slice the fish open and remove the bones.

Bradley was mesmerized watching her work. She sliced her sharp stone along the fish's belly as if she'd done this a thousand times.

"Did you sneak into the cockpit?" he asked. He couldn't see how since the door had been right in front of him.

"All you need to survive is water, food, shelter, and a way to defend yourself." She demonstrated how to throw the spear. "That'll buy you time."

"You're not going to tell me, are you?"

"Eat up."

"You have a twin sister," he guessed. But that didn't explain how she knew him.

She smiled. Threads of moonlight reflected in her eyes, giving her a wraithlike appearance. She handed him half of a fish. "Eat before your friends return."

"They're not my friends."

"Obviously."

Bradley sniffed at the fish. It had a strong, oily odor. He turned up his nose at eating uncooked fish.

Like his mom used to, Monique encouraged him to eat up. It didn't taste like the cans of tuna his dad forced him to eat. He swallowed quickly because Monique was almost finished.

As they ate, pinpoints of light moved around the island from the beach where they'd fished, up over the crown, and toward the first beach. Now they moved toward the cliff.

"Time to go," she said.

"Shouldn't we rescue the co-pilot?"

"We can't. They moved her."

"What about Jake," Bradley asked, "the one who ran after you?"

Monique wiped her hands on a leafy bush and scrambled down the vine over their cave.

Bradley counted three lights—no two. One was a single stick with lights on both ends. Malcolm had all the lights and yelled at what looked like three figures dragging something uphill toward the cliff.

Moonlight shifted. No, the boys did. Tony the Joker was dragging something. Rick's glasses reflected the light. He and Jon pulled something else. Despite being terrified, Bradley wanted a better look.

"Psst." Monique's voice came from the cliff's edge.

He crawled and looked down in time to see her scoot into the cave. He was thankful he couldn't see the rocks below. He started down and hung on the ledge until the lights approached the clearing. The boys were dragging two bodies. Jon dropped Coach Mack's head.

Malcolm shoved Jon to the ground. "Listen, you fat pig. Pick him up."

Tony dragged Miguel by the arms. The head hung like a floppy dishrag. "Do we have to do this? It's not funny anymore."

"Yeah, you have to. Get moving." Malcolm shined his light toward the cliff's edge.

* * *

Bradley slid down the vines and climbed into the cave. The moment he was inside, light shined over the cliff at the breaking waves. His stomach heaved at the thought that he'd been climbing down the cliff, above the bodies of the pilot, Danny, and two other boys.

"I have something for you," Monique said.

For a moment he'd forgotten she was there. He didn't want her to see him this way, helpless as a newborn baby. He swallowed hard and pulled away from the opening.

She sat across from him. Malcolm's light off the cliff reflected shadows on her face. She put a finger to her lips and pointed up. Then she handed Bradley a large bronze coin. He moved closer to the opening to see it better. The coin was an award for excellence in mountain climbing. He felt ashamed that he didn't know as much about how to survive as she did.

"Thanks," he whispered.

She covered her mouth and wagged her finger at him. He nodded. Malcolm was above them.

"He's too heavy." Jon's strained voice came from outside.

"You should exercise more," Malcolm said. "Drag him over to the edge."

Through the ivy, Bradley saw part of the cliff face nearby. Afraid of being seen, he drew back.

"Pick it up," Malcolm said.

"Shouldn't we say something," Jon said. "He was our coach."

Bradley flinched as Coach Mack's body fell past the opening. Jon let loose a curdling scream. Coach hit the rocks with a thud. Jon fell past the opening, his arms flailing. He cried out and gurgled.

"Jon?" Rick said. "Why'd you do that? You're crazy. No! NO!"

"Crazy, huh," Malcolm said. "We'll see about that."

He must have pushed Rick. The smaller boy screamed all the way to the rocks below. Bradley wanted to look and not look at the same time. He didn't want to be next.

"You didn't have to do that," Tony said. "He wasn't going to tell anyone."

"Now he won't for sure," Malcolm said. "Let's find our Little Worm. He has to be around here somewhere."

"We should look for Rick," Tony said.

"Not until we have Bradley."

* * *

Bradley waited until the voices above faded away. Then he poked his head out of the cave into darkness. Waves broke against the rocks below. He couldn't see the bodies. He'd lost track of how many were there.

For the longest time he strained to see, until his eyes ached as much as his heart. He hated feeling helpless. He hadn't stood up for Danny. He hadn't tried to stop Malcolm from pushing Rick and Jon over the cliff. He couldn't even save the co-pilot.

He settled into the cave, no longer able to feel Monique's presence. Being alone in the dark spooked him.

Bradley forced air into his lungs, stale with whatever had lived and decayed in this cave. He hoped it was birds or small mammals, something that wouldn't harm him. But the odor of the cave mixed with the smell of the fish to make him feel it was coming from the bodies on the rocks below. He didn't want to be alone on a night like this. He certainly didn't want Malcolm hurting Monique.

He felt his way around the cave to the tunnel. Dragging his spear with him, he crawled along the foul tunnel to the pit. Moving made him feel less helpless.

Monique wasn't in the pit when he got there. There was no sound of anyone nearby, so he climbed the rocky side of the pit and hid in the bushes. The clouds had thinned, allowing moonlight to poke through.

A single light lit up Tony's face and moved from the cliff down toward the pit. Then it disappeared. Either that or Tony had turned it off. The light reappeared, moving down toward Bradley. He dropped lower to the ground and was plunged into darkness.

When he looked up, a brighter double light hung near the cockpit, not moving. Bradley held tight to his spear and prepared to jump into the pit. Moonlight caught Monique's curls. She appeared on a ledge above him as if she could see him clear as daylight. She held out her spear, turned, and hurried up toward the cliff.

Bradley carried his spear like a walking stick and followed. Monique ran, disappearing ahead of him. He reached the top of the hill. The cliff was to his right. The double light was not far from where the cockpit had landed.

Not seeing Monique or the single light anywhere, he moved toward the cockpit, curious as to why the double-light hadn't moved. Malcolm was hunting him, the Little Worm, yet he wasn't moving. Was he lying in wait?

Bradley slid down a slippery patch and stepped on something soft and squishy. When he looked down he gasped and fell backward into bushes.

Tony the Joker was face down, a stake through his chest. In the moonlight, it looked like one of his comical pranks, except blood pooled around his shirt. The stake looked like it broke off a spear. *Monique?*

Not knowing whether to be impressed or petrified, Bradley was both. She'd been there when Jake had disappeared as well. His heart raced, jumping into his throat. She was a mountain girl. She'd given him the medallion so he would know. She knew how to survive out here.

* * *

Bradley heard groaning nearby. Trembling, he shook loose from his imaginings. He held the spear as Monique had showed him and moved toward the light. Up ahead, poking out from the shadows along the path, he saw blonde curls on the ground. He tasted vomit. The spear shook in his hand. Still, he moved closer and listened for Monique's screams.

She didn't make a sound. But Malcolm did, grunting with exertion, his hands around the blonde's neck.

Gripping his only weapon, Bradley inched forward. He imagined Danny after he stopped screaming. And the others. *No!*

As if possessed by the devil herself, Bradley charged into the light. "Leave her alone, you monster." He looked down to where the blonde lay, but couldn't see Monique through his tears.

Malcolm rolled away from the body and stood up. "Little Worm grows a spine. You think that makes you a man?"

Bradley's trembling hand shook the spear. His eyes burned. He wiped them and started to charge the bigger boy. "Be a man," his father would say.

Malcolm raised a stick. "Argh." He jumped up and down, puffing out his chest like a baboon.

"Run. Get out of here," Bradley yelled to Monique.

"She's not going anywhere and neither are you," Malcolm said. "It's just you and me. Man and Worm." He threw the stick, hitting Bradley's bruised arm.

Stepping back, Bradley fell over debris. He steadied himself, trying to recall what Monique had said about holding and throwing the spear. He would only get one shot. His hands were shaking too much to aim well.

"I'm going to enjoy tearing you to pieces, Little Worm." Malcolm picked up another stick and threw it.

Bradley ducked. "Run," he shouted to Monique. "Hide somewhere."

"There's nowhere to hide on this tiny island. That's the beauty of it. You're as good as dead."

"You can't scare me," Bradley said.

The sly smile returned to Malcolm's face. "You'll still die like the others. Poor scared Little Worm."

Malcolm threw a stone, hitting Bradley's head. When Malcolm bent over to pick up something else to throw, Bradley threw the spear. It grazed Malcolm's back and slid away. Bradley ran toward the cliff.

Malcolm was right. Bradley didn't know how to fight. He wasn't a killer. Yet if he didn't end this, Malcolm would.

Bradley didn't want to give up the hideout, but if he didn't get away from Malcolm, it wouldn't matter. He tried to locate where to climb down.

The bigger boy gave chase. "You can't hide from me. No one can. Stop and I'll let you be my slave for the night." He was gaining on the Little Worm.

Outlined by rays of moonlight, Monique knelt on the cliff. She climbed over the edge. She'd gotten away. But it made no sense. She was motionless on the ground. Malcolm was hurting her. Now he was after the Little Worm.

Bradley etched the spot in his mind where Monique had knelt and ran as fast as he could.

"Where you going, Little Worm? You going to jump? Maybe you should."

Bradley found the spot, dropped to the ground, and grabbed hold of the vines. Malcolm was a mere ten feet behind. On the ground behind the brute was a head with blonde curls. That had to be the co-pilot.

Bradley shimmied down to the cave entrance. As soon as he had his feet on the ledge leading into their hideout, light blazed down from above. He dropped down another foot and tried to remember how he'd climbed in before.

Malcolm set the light down and began to cut at the ivy with the knife he'd taken from Miguel. Bradley lifted his feet and swung them over the ledge and into the cave entrance. Malcolm stopped cutting to throw stones. Bradley flinched and dodged aside. Before he fell onto the rocks below, he pulled himself into the cave. The last thing he saw before he was inside was Malcolm grabbing the vines to climb down.

"You can't escape," Malcolm said. "I've got you now, scared Little Worm."

Bradley crawled backward into the cave. Once he was inside, Monique handed him her spear. Nodding, he braced himself and grabbed hold of the weapon. He placed the point toward the entrance as Malcolm rappelled down the vines. First came the feet. Then the big boy's face hung over the opening. He shined a light inside and stared at the spear.

"You're not man enough," Malcolm said.

Trembling, Bradley jabbed the point at the bigger boy.

Malcolm kicked away from the cliff to avoid the strike. The force of his push and his weight snapped the partly-cut vines. Scrambling up the falling stems, he let the light tumble to the rocks below. He wailed like a baby all the way down. His landing came with a thud and sounded like the snapping of twigs.

Bradley peered down at waves breaking over the rocks, lit by a double-sided light. Malcolm stared up with vacant eyes. His right arm twitched as if he were shaking his fist. Then it stopped. Around him were eleven other bodies.

* * *

Bradley withdrew into the cave. Monique was gone. He liked how strong and tomboyish she was, though not how she disappeared, leaving him alone. He didn't go after her. He'd had far too much excitement for one day, for a lifetime. Besides, she knew how to get by in the wild. He curled up by the cave entrance with the spear in his hand and kept watch until his eyes refused to stay open.

He woke to light entering the cave. Monique sat, watching him. He got up and bumped his head, which hurt from the night before. He rubbed his scalp but the real ache was inside.

"It's time for you to go," she said.

"Go where?"

"A helicopter landed. They're searching for survivors."

"They found us?" he said. "That's great. Wait, aren't you coming?"

"I can't. But you should hurry before they leave."

"The vine is gone."

"The tunnel," she said. "Come on. I'll see you off."

"We've only just met."

She smiled. "That's sweet. Now go."

Bradley followed her through the tunnel and out of the pit. The smell didn't bother him now that it was daylight and rescuers had come. Dozens of men and women in bright orange uniforms spread out searching.

"I'll never forget you," Monique said. "Go. It would be best if you didn't tell them about me."

"Are you …"

"Am I what?"

"Malcolm said you were a she-devil," Bradley said.

"What do you think?" She pointed toward the beach.

"I don't want to leave. I like you."

"Go on, no more fuss." She dropped into the pit. "Go."

Before Bradley could jump in after her, an orange uniformed arm grabbed him.

"Careful there," a man's voice said. He pulled Bradley away from the pit. "You got a name, son?"

"Bradley Munsch." He eyed the pit, but Monique had vanished.

"I'm Captain Tunney. We're here to take you home."

Bradley shrugged. He didn't want to go home to a father who thought him a sissy. He wanted to stay with Monique.

"We would have arrived sooner," the captain grumbled, "but the plane's transponder and black box stopped signaling. Luckily, we were able to triangulate off a cell phone signal. Where is everyone?"

Bradley's gut churned. He couldn't stop trembling at the memories. "Malcolm dumped bodies off the cliff."

"Malcolm Jones?"

Bradley nodded.

The captain put his arm around the boy. "Where is he now?"

Shivering at the memory, Bradley pointed toward the cliff. "You have to save my friend, Monique."

"Monique? Why don't you slow down and start at the beginning."

* * *

Bradley finished telling Captain Tunney his story.

"So you're the only survivor?" the captain asked.

"I tried to bandage the co-pilot," Bradley said, recalling her broken arm, "but Malcolm found her."

"I'm sorry. Being alone during all this must have been quite upsetting."

"I had Monique."

A soldier with sergeant stripes approached. "You've got to see this." He pointed up toward the cliff.

"The boy told me. Any survivors?"

The sergeant shook his head. "We've scoured the island using infrared and motion sensors."

"What about Monique?" Bradley asked. "She has to be here."

"There's no one by that name on the passenger list," the soldier said. "And we've accounted for thirteen boys and four adults."

"I swear. She's here," Bradley said. "I think she's Coach McDonald's daughter."

"McDonald and your co-pilot have a daughter named Megan," the captain said. "No Monique."

That twisted Bradley's innards. He choked to think of Megan wanting to come with her parents and losing them both. Tears filled his eyes. Then it hit him. Monique had to be Megan. She knew him and he'd seen her at the airport. She was the girl Malcolm said was Coach's daughter. "Maybe she snuck into the cockpit."

"No room," the captain said. "Look, we need to get you home."

"But Monique?"

"Excuse me." Captain Tunney took the sergeant uphill, away from Bradley, and whispered. "Between the crash and hiding from Malcolm Jones, we shouldn't be surprised the boy has become delusional about an imaginary friend."

Bradley's ears perked up as the winds blew his way.

"I'll keep an eye on him," the sergeant said.

"Thanks."

"Is it true what they're saying that there's a warrant for Malcolm's arrest, for assaulting a woman yesterday?"

The captain nodded. "Allegedly he attacked the social worker checking up on a report that Malcolm had put his own mother in the hospital last month."

"Maybe it's a blessing he's gone."

"Except now we won't get answers.

* * *

79

The sergeant buckled Bradley into one of two military helicopters on the beach where the fuselage had come to rest.

Bradley wanted to find Monique, but she didn't want to be found. And she knew how to hide. That made him smile. She'd saved his life. He owed her. If that meant letting her go, he had to give her that.

Through the open door, he overheard two orange-uniformed soldiers talking outside.

"What did you say they call this island?" one soldier asked.

"An Aussie named it Sheila Rock," another soldier said. "Some call it She-devil Rocks. Quite a few boats have crashed on these shores. There's no fresh water. No one can live here for long."

"So Malcolm went on a rampage before falling off the cliff last night."

"Looks like it," the second soldier said. "If I had to wager, I'd say he caused this crash to avoid getting arrested. Then he killed himself. I do find it curious that one of the boys fell into a ravine, stabbing himself on the branch of a thorny bush and another fell into a pit, breaking his neck.

"She-devil Rocks about sums it up, then."

As they lifted off, Bradley plastered his face against the window. The island was small with a few trees, scrubby vegetation, and few places to hide. Except Monique had found water, food, and a cave to escape Malcolm. Bradley felt terrible that he couldn't save the co-pilot. If Monique was Megan then his new friend had lost both her parents.

Monique had been the best friend he'd ever had.

The helicopter lifted and flew south. Bradley spotted a lone figure on the cliff. Her blond hair blew in the wind. She held a spear in each hand, which she raised in salute.

He started to point her out for the sergeant but decided against turning her in. As he shifted in his seat, the medallion dug into his leg. He reached into his pocket and clutched the token Monique had given him.

I will return for you.

■ ■ ■

MAIDEN VOYAGE
(Space opera thriller)

Nina Rekovic Private Log 2098-10-17/8:06 AM

Another security sweep and another boring diversion from my Chief Engineer duties. In the five years since we left Earth's orbit, it's been mostly crimes of boredom: squabbles over limited space and who-did-what-to-or-with-whom.

In the orange com-room I find my sweetie, Chief Communications Officer Carmen Blythe. Her lithe, muscular form jerks to attention when I enter. She's been dozing again: end of shift.

I push aside her brown curls and massage her knotted shoulders. She leans forward to give me room to loosen the muscles across her well-toned back. Being on opposing shifts, I rarely see her, like ghosts passing at twilight. Her shift ends as mine begins. At least I can time my security sweeps to catch her before she gets off. She rises; gives me a welcome hug and a lingering kiss: implied promises for the weekend.

Lucky me, at least I get to move on my rounds. Carmen has to sit and listen to intermittent Earth-coms that now take a year to reach us. The rarely used QE-com light flashes and squawks static that could wake the dead.

Carmen pulls away. "Got-to-go." She looks like she's been studying all night for com finals and needs an adrenaline boost.

I should get on with my rounds, but I linger. It feels good to hang with Carmen and watch her work. She's the reason I signed onto the Maiden's Ark after my dad's prolonged brain cancer got the better of him. He refused advanced treatments; he didn't want to artificially prolong his life.

Quantum-Entanglement-coms are unusual. To provide their limited instantaneous communications, Captain Belova McDaniels—I call her Beluga because of her size—installed two QE containment units. The first entangles with a sister unit in Colorado Springs; the other on the miss-named 'dark' side of the moon, the side facing away from Earth.

Carmen runs the QE signal through filters to verify consistency and reconstruct the message from the few bits of transmitted data. This much I've gathered from scattered weekend conversations over drinks. She has to tease out the message before its delicate quantum bits are lost.

I tremble with excitement. The last QE-com two years ago announced election results: Neanderthals won. Actually, real Neanderthals would have been an improvement. The election only reinforced Captain McDaniel's rationale for leaving the Earth behind and starting a new life.

Of course it took over seven months for the regular Earth-com details to arrive. The Radical Patriot's Party had won by promising to gut the space budget as they took a machete to all "non-essential" government programs.

Three words scroll across Carmen's screen:

Earth lost asteroid.

"What does it mean?" I ask. Mention of asteroids triggers memories of my ex-boyfriend and his asteroid mining operations, which were more important to him than I was. Carmen helped me pick up the pieces when he left one day without saying goodbye.

She looks up as if she just notices me. "They lost an asteroid? Why send that message?"

"That's it?"

Carmen shakes her head while probing the message. "The rest is … gibberish." She works frantically at her controls. "Not good. The helium atoms split."

I shut up, let her concentrate, and try to make sense of the cryptic message and how unnerved Carmen is. I've never seen her so anxious. I hold my breath until she finishes. When she pushes away from the controls, she digs her fingers into her scalp, grabbing clumps of brown hair. I try to hold her, but she pulls away and does a mad crazy dance in the middle of the orange com-room. She's hyperventilating and yet her tan skin has gone pale.

"What is it, Hon?"

She catches her breath. "Earth's gone! Has to be."

Carmen spins around as if searching for her anchor, but when I approach, she pushes me away. Eyes narrow; she regains focus. "It would take a nuke to split helium like that. I had to jettison the QE-unit before the containment field collapsed and destroyed our ship."

"We can't communicate with Earth anymore?"

"I don't think there's an Earth to communicate with."

"What about the moon base?" I ask.

Carmen drops into her seat and activates the moon's QE-com. I don't want to wait the year it will take for regular electromagnetic signals to reach our Earth-com to confirm what happened. How is this even possible?

I struggle to breathe. I knew signing onto the Maiden's Ark meant never returning to Earth, never being able to visit Dad's grave again. But the thought that his grave might be gone slams my gut, sending its contents in both directions. I steady myself to control the urges.

"This'll take time," Carmen says. "Assuming moon folk are even watching after what happened."

Focus, I tell myself. *I'm Chief of Security.* "We have to tell the captain and the passengers."

Carmen gets up and blocks the door. Her hazel eyes narrow, while her voice descends into a harsh whisper. "Tell no one. Nod that you understand."

I back away. "What's going on? People deserve to know."

"Know what? That we got a garbled message?"

"You said—"

"Keep your mouth shut," Carmen says. "You weren't even supposed to be here."

"Captain McDaniels named me Chief of Security." I almost say Beluga because after years under her thumb, I can't stand our big-boned leader.

Carmen's face softens. When she moves aside, Beluga fills the doorway. I hold my tongue and look up into her dark eyes, which don't meet mine. While I support the captain's mission to start a new civilization with only women, I have growing reservations over her dictatorship. The Maiden's Ark Covenant gives us no recourse. I swallow my reservations and step back.

She enters and closes the door. "Show me the message."

Earth lost asteroid scrolls across the screen.

"Erase it," the captain says.

I interrupt, "Shouldn't we let the crew and passengers—"

"We're not stirring things up for a cryptic message we can't verify for a year. Besides, there's nothing we can do."

"What if survivors need our help?" I ask.

"We don't change plans based on garbled messages. We don't even know if there are survivors. We'll wait until regular channels come through."

"That'll take over a year."

"So be it. Earth's catastrophe, if that's what it is, makes our mission even more critical."

I want to say more, but Carmen's eyes narrow: *shut up*. I nod, though I'm not okay with this. For all I know, the women on board the Maiden's Ark may be all that remain of the human race.

The last regular Earth-com I know of came in yesterday, sent a year ago. It sounded desperate: riots, famine, terror attacks. It was enough to make me glad I'd left. Yet I feel an ache to return and do whatever's possible to help out. Now all our petty squabbles seemed just that—petty.

But Carmen isn't supposed to share Earth-coms with me, so I don't say anything. I don't want the captain mad at her.

The captain turns to me. "Aren't you late for your rounds? You're not on holiday."

I nod, and reach for the door.

Beluga grabs my wrist. "Not a word to anyone."

* * *

Nina Rekovic Private Log 2098-10-17/9:56 AM

The Maiden's Ark with its quarter million women and girls is like a huge high school. Fifty deck levels spread out with twenty-five hundred apartments on each level in a grid of fifty by fifty. I cover some twenty miles of teal-tinted residential corridors using my implanted Eye-pad viewer while I head to the yellow commons on deck fifty, with its stores, exercise facilities, and cafeteria. If I'm going to play cop, might as well have my mid-morning donut—a soy-algae substitute that tries. At least it's not fattening. I don't need Carmen getting on my case.

Our Chief Cook, olive-skinned Francesca Giovanni, greets me with a tray of my favorites. They all taste the same. She makes an effort by giving these a floral rainbow coloring—natural algae tones, of course.

"You look like end of shift," Francesca says. "You up all night?"

I shake my head. "Focused on my Eye-pad too long."

She laughs.

It takes all my self-control not to tell Francesca what I've learned. I need to tell someone. To let out this ache inside me that there's really no going back. I pray for some other explanation, but Carmen was definite. One of our QE-coms is gone, severed forever. I steel my nerves—can't let on.

Unlike me, Francesca left people behind and regrets "getting tricked" into signing on. When she broke up with her philandering husband, one of Beluga's faithful befriended her. Like joining a religious cult Francesca got all the surround-love she needed. Before she knew it, she was on the Maiden's Ark.

Now she's one of the Returners who want to turn this ship around and go home. She wasn't one of the twelve who signed the petition four years ago and spent six months in lockup. There were many like her who sympathized, but refused to sign. Some of Maiden's Ark most devout colonists said we should pack all the Returners on a shuttle and send them back, but with insufficient supplies: a death sentence. Thankfully Beluga didn't agree, though I suspect she didn't want to lose one of her shuttles.

I can't say I blame the Returners. At twenty percent of light speed, we don't expect to reach the blue-green planet QX-22864 for another hundred-and-twenty years. By that time most of us who began this journey will be dead. This was all in the fine print.

"No chance of turning this boat around is there?" she asks for the thousandth time.

I force a smile. Yeah, but I can't tell you unless I want to spend six months recycling human waste down in lockup.

"No disturbances this morning?" I ask.

"The usual: two restless girls started a food fight, three teens complained about bland food. I do my best."

"I know you do. You want me to investigate?"

"I took care of it. Get your head back into engineering, where you belong."

She knows I don't like security. I make my way down the lift to engineering on level fourteen, eating the soy-algae pastries on the way. At the same time, I scan all the common areas on other levels on my Eye-pad. While I don't see anything to worry about, many of these women would be upset if they knew. Captain Beluga is right. Why get them riled up when there's nothing they can do. We'll keep getting messages for another year. Then we'll have real answers.

When I reach the white hallway lined with engineering rooms, I bump into my blonde Senior Engineer Zola Cohen. I offer her the remaining donut. I want to tell her what happened to her family on Earth, for the sake of her and her reclusive teenage daughter Magdalena, but her pinched face seems intent on something else.

"Problems?" I ask.

"Nothing I can't handle. I left reports on your desk."

I want to ask why she didn't forward them to my Eye-pad, but she hurries down the sterile corridor. I move to my desk and go through the usual problems: damage to a forward shield, clogged air-cleansing unit, adjustments to recycling tanks. When Captain Beluga named me Chief of Security, I put Zola in charge of engineering during my absences. She's done fine without me.

I guess I'm expendable.

* * *

Nina Rekovic Private Log 2098-10-17/4:43 PM

Tired of reports and budgets, I start my afternoon security sweep by checking on the whereabouts of my sweetie. I want to see her, but I also want to know what the moon's QE-com revealed. I locate Carmen entering Captain Beluga's office, yuck. In fairness, the captain isn't ugly. She's just bigger than most women, and has a commanding voice and intimidating personality. She also has the Covenant making her Empress of this realm.

After scanning residential corridors and commons, nothing concerning, I stop off at the darkened observation lounge on forty-nine. Two couples are making out under the stars. It makes me think of Carmen, though she doesn't like public displays of affection. I finish my rounds and find her in the blue wing on forty-nine, sitting at the bar with two of her com techies. They're all dressed in floral leisure gowns. She changed. I sit beside her on an elevated seat that adjusts to my height and weight.

She pushes some blue-green concoction my way. "Try it. Something new."

I take a sip; enjoy tingling around my mouth before it goes down. Like all "drinks" on board, the alcohol content is severely limited. It also contains a mild sedative to keep drinkers from getting rowdy. Carmen is already zoning out. She should be catching up on sleep, but the Earth communication must be troubling her.

Wanting answers, I escort her along blue corridors, through the yellow commons, down the lift to seven and along our residential hallway.

"You could have stayed for drinks," Carmen says. "Try to be sociable."

She leans into me until I get her into the apartment. After I open the door, she stumbles into the bedroom and plops onto the bed, fully clothed. I've missed her awake-time. Now it's time for her beauty rest. But if I sleep now, I'll be up during her shift with nothing I want to do.

"Come on, you're not sleeping in your leisure gown."

She gets up. "I don't need a nursemaid." She looks alert; then stumbles to the wall-dresser and stands there.

I steady her. "What was in the moon's QE-com?"

She pulls away. "Lunar confirmed: Two asteroids collided. Debris hit Earth. Coms lost. Volcanic activity. Thick clouds."

"What about our moon colonies?"

"Earth-side gone. Five thousand on far side survived, plus asteroid miners."

"Was this a terrorist attack?"

Carmen shakes her head, her expression grim. "No way to know."

"The lunar colony can't survive without resupply," I say.

"I know. Plus, Earth's orbit may have altered. We're trying to calculate."

"We have to tell the others. We have to go back."

Carmen straightens up as if from a jolt of adrenaline. She places her hand on my cheek, almost a slap. "Tell no one. If this goes public, it'll stir up Returners. We're not going back."

I remove her hand. "What's gotten into you? Survivors will need our help."

"As Chief of Security, your job is to maintain peace, not to stir up trouble."

"Don't lecture me."

Carmen pushes past me. "Don't cross the captain."

"What's that supposed to mean?" I follow her to the door. "And where are you going?"

"Not your concern. Don't follow."

She slips out into the corridor and slams the door.

I want to call her back, but not for another fight. I let her go.

* * *

Nina Rekovic Private Log 2098-10-18/8:18 AM

On my way to visit Carmen in the com-room as part of my morning security sweep, I scan my Eye-pad. On almost every level, small groups whisper in yellow corridors.

Am I being paranoid or has word gotten out?

I shake it off. Common areas attract cliques gossiping about who's sleeping with whom and who did what to their best friend.

When I enter the orange com-room, Carmen isn't happy to see me.

I close the door. "I missed you last night." *A lot.*

Actually, I miss the Carmen I knew on Earth, the one I gave up everything to follow onboard. Back then we had candlelight dinners by the river and took walks. Now all we do is avoid each other and fight. I sigh.

Carmen's hazel eyes narrow as if she doesn't know me. "You had to do it, didn't you?"

"Do what?"

"Who did you tell?"

I back against the wall. "Not a soul."

"Don't tell me you didn't notice Returners gossiping."

"Just the usual."

Captain Beluga enters the com-room without knocking and towers over me. "We have a problem."

"Carmen was briefing me," I say, trying to get in front of her challenge.

The captain frowns, wrinkling her large forehead. She shakes her head. "I just came from the fertility lab. Someone sabotaged our EggFusion apparatus. I don't have to tell you what that means. Or who is responsible."

I struggle to breathe. The future of our all-female society, maybe the entire human race, depends on the success of EggFusion Fertilization, the ability to fertilize one woman's egg with another woman's cells. Without it, we're extinct in a generation. "You think Returners did this?"

"Who else?"

"Couldn't it be a malfunction? I'll get my engineers—"

"Zola's working on it. I want you to round up all Returners for questioning. Quarantine them until I decide how to deal with this."

"We can't—"

"This is a terrorist attack! Under Article Nine, Section Twenty-Three of the Maiden's Ark Covenant, I hereby order you to imprison all suspects, which means all Returners. You may deputize whoever you need to assist. Take them to Deck A."

That's next to recycling.

I look to Carmen who returns to her seat, and another Lunar QE-com.

* * *

Nina Rekovic Private Log 2098-10-18/8:58 AM

I know most of the Returners, having talked them down from despair. It doesn't seem fair to use that knowledge and confidences against them. Yet someone had jeopardized our future. If I arrest them, I'm a skunk. If I don't, I'm a traitor.

There's nothing in my inbox from Zola, which annoys me. I message her to tell me the instant she learns anything. Then I hurry down yellow corridors to visit Francesca. She greets me with her soy-algae donuts, all smiles. "New flavor today."

I hold up my hands. I can't accept these and then arrest her. "You heard about the fertility lab?"

She drops the donuts on a nearby table. "Terrible business. I hope you catch whoever did this."

I sigh. "Captain's orders. I have to quarantine all Returners."

"I see." Offering no resistance, she holds her hands behind for me to cuff.

"I was hoping you'd help me gather them peacefully. I'd like to deputize you."

"Me?" Francesca says. "I'm just a crotchety old woman, all talk. Are the rumors about Earth true?" She lowers her voice. "Or is that so Returners will stop griping?"

"Francesca, please. I don't want anyone getting hurt. This is serious."

"People trust you. Now you're betraying them?"

"I'm not a priest or a lawyer," I say. "Nothing told to me is privileged, not when it involves the safety of this ship."

"Very well," Francesca says. "But only to make sure no one gets hurt."

We don't even have to go hunting for Returners. Three young women from electronics fabrication join us, still in tight brown work uniforms. "Is it true what they say?" the supervisor asks.

"Was it nuclear war?" the youngest asks.

"Are there any survivors?"

I look up at camera locations and shake my head. "We can't talk here."

I lead the three fabricators toward lifts in the middle of the commons. Francesca joins me. The betrayal tears at my guts. Yet the last thing I want is rebellion on this fragile vessel, our entire world.

"We're going back for survivors, aren't we?" the youngest fabricator asks.

Two seamstresses from the clothing shop join us as we enter the lift. "Tell us it isn't true," one says.

I pull them into the lift and activate for Deck A. "You know gossip and rumors can get you into trouble." *And me.* I eye Francesca who closes her eyes.

When we reach Deck A, there's that ghastly aroma of recycling: urine tanks, feces mulching, food decomposition, and medical decontamination. I force myself not to make a face. I need to set a good example.

"Yuck," the young seamstress says. "Where are we?"

I pull Francesca with me down a gray corridor to the dungeon, the ship's jail, while keeping a watchful eye that the others follow. She's like the Pied Piper. People follow without asking questions. That further tugs at my guilt.

We reach a gray steel door, which opens to my implant. That makes me wonder if Captain Beluga might cancel my authorization once I'm inside. I push those thoughts aside and lead three fabricators and two seamstresses into the hold. When the gray door seals behind us, the recycling smell fades.

A second gray door opens. Sergeant Kyra Yost stands along the wall with her MTT weapon drawn. The Multi-Tasking Taser is capable of immobilizing each or all seven of us. Francesca presses herself against the wall as I nudge the fabricators forward.

"What's this all about?" the fabrication supervisor says. "I thought you'd give us answers."

I urge the two seamstresses toward Yost and turn to the supervisor. "Captain's orders. There was a terror attack. Captain suspects Returners."

The fabricators look at each other. "What attack?" the supervisor asks.

"I'm sorry. Until we find the saboteurs, Captain wants you to wait down here."

"We're under arrest?"

"Detention, for your own good," I say. "We don't want anyone seeking vengeance, do we?"

"What about Earth?" the supervisor asks.

"Until we know—"

"That's bull."

"I'll check back later," I say.

The supervisor grabs my arm. Francesca intervenes. "Let go."

"You're working with her?" the supervisor asks Francesca

"We'll get to the bottom of this. Nina is right. I've heard a lot of anger this morning."

"It's all lies," the supervisor says. "Lies. You hear me."

I wait until Sergeant Yost has the Returners locked up and lead Francesca back down the gray corridor.

"What if Returners didn't do this?" she asks.

"Who then? If EggFusion fails, we're doomed. Who would want that?"

"Returners don't."

"Most, maybe," I say. "But that fabrication supervisor is pretty angry."

* * *

Nina Rekovic Private Log 2098-10-18/12:22 PM

We reach the last of the Returners, two couples from the Ag Facility, in the commons on level forty-eight. Several angry women corner them, yelling, "Traitors."

I have one hand on my stun gun, praying I don't have to use it. Seeing Francesca, the angry crowd turns on her. She joins the Ag workers to comfort them.

I stand where I can see them all. "Listen to me. Get back to your stations. Captain's orders: I'm taking these four to lockup."

"They've destroyed our future," Delilah Witherspoon says. The fiery redhead has caused me trouble before.

"I doubt Ag workers had anything to do with it. They don't have access." I don't mention that they could easily tamper with food to create havoc.

The redhead gets into my face. "You're one of them. That's why."

I've seen her get physical with other women, which has me wanting to step back, but I stand my ground. "You want a week in lockup?"

"Screw you." She turns to the other women. "Let them suffer with the recycling waste."

When Delilah leads her rabble away, I join Francesca and the Ag workers. "You okay?"

"Thanks," a pretty brunette says. "I thought they'd lynch us. Do we have to go to lockup? We promise to stay in our rooms. You could have us monitored."

"Captain's orders, for your own protection."

Francesca frowns.

"We didn't do anything," the brunette says.

"I believe you. Please come quietly."

Francesca nods and the Ag women comply.

After Sergeant Yost takes them to their cells, Francesca grabs my arm. "I'm staying to make sure they're okay. Find out what's going on, and watch your back."

"I need your help up there."

"I'd be a target and a distraction. Good luck."

* * *

Nina Rekovic Private Log 2098-10-18/3:08 PM

I've missed the entire day in engineering and haven't heard from Zola. I swing by to find the pinched-face blonde at my desk, getting too comfortable in my absence.

No time for jealousies.

"What have you learned?"

Zola jumps out of my seat and stands back. "Just keeping things going."

"And your report?"

"Captain stopped by and took it. She said not to distract you; that you were working on delicate, confidential business."

"What about your findings?" I try to contain my irritation.

"Right. Whoever did this knew enough about electronics to incapacitate the EFF units. They're fried."

"Can you rebuild them?"

My other Senior Engineer enters. "Hey, Zol—" Jen's tanned round face shows surprise framed by puffy black curls. She blushes and leaves, making me wonder what else is going on.

Later.

"Not sure," Zola says. "It was tricky equipment to begin with—eighty percent failure rates."

"What about the backup unit?"

"Also fried. Professional job."

"How soon can you determine if we can fix this?" I ask.

Zola moves away from my desk, toward the door. "I need a day or two to come up with a plan."

"Make sure I see it first."

She nods. "Will do, boss."

I head toward the fertility lab on twelve; have to see for myself. On my Eye-Pad I see clusters of women arguing. Using my wrist-com, I link the sound to my ear implants and hear them talk about the roundup of Returners and rumors about Earth.

Only the captain, Carmen, and I knew, and I told no one. This could get ugly if I don't figure out who's behind the sabotage and the leak. We should have told the passengers up front.

"Put them on a shuttle and send them home," a voice yells as I pass through the cafeteria. I turn to see the redhead. "Kick them off this ark."

"Kill them, in other words. Is that what we stand for?"

"They shouldn't have signed on."

"Some were tricked."

The redhead backs away when she sees I'm still operating as Security Chief with my hand on my stun gun. I can imagine what she'll say behind my back. Captain wants a troublemaker; I'd nominate her. I keep moving.

It's like high school, where I was odd girl out. I try to forget, but watching cliques, alliances, politicking, and back-stabbing brings back sour memories.

I'm surprised when I reach the fertility lab to find doors open and lights out. I activate the switch and try to close the doors. They're jammed.

Sergeant Wynona Tucker jumps out from one of the

examination rooms with her stun gun out. Seeing me, the stocky cop puts it down. "Captain assigned me because we can't lock the facilities. They busted this place up good."

I'm annoyed that Zola didn't mention the damage and Captain Beluga didn't inform me she was assigning my security team. "What have you learned?"

Tucker resets a silent alarm at the door. "Someone came in last night after the lab was locked. It looks to me like someone on the inside."

"Why do you say that?"

"Door wasn't forced. It was damaged after, to make it look like a break-in. They cut circuits to the lab and pulsed the equipment. That fried everything except the lights, which are on a different circuit." More that wasn't in Zola's brief report.

"What about cams?" I ask.

"Nothing."

"Erased?"

"No," Tucker says. "Timestamp shows no gaps and no activity. Whoever did this was well-informed and clever."

"So we're looking at someone who works in the lab, has access to our secured pulse weapons, and can tamper with the cams."

The sergeant nods and pushes back strands of brown hair.

"I don't suppose we have any real suspects."

"No, but it has to be someone who wants us to turn back."

"Keep digging. Next time give me a courtesy message that you've been assigned."

"Will do."

* * *

Nina Rekovic Private Log 2098-10-18/6:02 PM

What troubles me about the timing of the attack, after rumors spread about Earth, is that a non-Returner might have changed her mind. Anyone can be a suspect. I track Carmen to Crazy Eights Bar on level eight.

How original.

When I get there, she's plastered, as much as you can be on two percent alcohol and sedatives. I've never seen her this bad.

"Time to go home," I tell her.

"You don't own me."

That's the bone we keep fighting over. While we've lived

together for six years and she's the reason I came, she never wanted a commitment.

I rub her shoulders. "You should get some sleep."

Carmen pulls away. "Enough."

"Can we go talk somewhere?"

"You should move out."

That stings and draws attention from patrons who suddenly look alert and sober.

"I miss you," I whisper.

"Hey, you heard our friend," a crusty brunette yells. "Buzz off. You're spoiling our fun."

"Not so tough off the job." It's the redhead, Delilah. "Hey, everyone, our chief cop is a Returner sympathizer."

"I'm a peace officer," I say.

"Maybe you're the saboteur. After all, you have access to everything and you're friendly with Returners."

"Why don't you all go sleep this off?"

"Why don't you step outside?" The redhead stands before me with almost masculine features.

I look to Carmen, who in the past has stood by me. She stares at the counter and takes another drink. I signal Sergeants Yost and Tucker, leaving my com open. "One more word and I'll close Crazy Eights for the night and send the speaker down to Deck A."

I back up toward the door, making sure no one is behind me. It's something I've noticed over the past few months, something that crept up on me. A few of the women, the redhead in particular, have taken on aggressive masculine behavior.

Nature abhors a vacuum.

* * *

Nina Rekovic Private Log 2098-10-18/7:13 PM

While I make my way down teal corridors to my apartment, I scan my Eye-Pad for other bar activity. Looks like the sabotage and rumors of Earth have everyone on edge. I'll have to ask the captain for more security if this keeps up. But there are few I'd trust. Francesca is in lockup and Carmen isn't talking to me. Issues with my roommate/partner—I'm not sure which—have been brewing for some time. I can't keep ignoring them.

Absent her, I'm a Returner. But sabotage isn't the answer.

The Maiden's Ark is a fragile vessel despite the best technology

Captain McDonald could buy. It reminds me of the Titanic, the unsinkable vessel until it wasn't. The fertility sabotage was a blow, a wake-up call that internal conflict could doom us. It's hard enough to get a dozen people to work together let alone a quarter million, yet we have to settle our differences peacefully. And, we have to go back for the sake of the human race, to help survivors, and because ignoring their plight diminishes us as human beings.

My implant triggers my apartment door to open. I go in before I realize I'm not alone. The short, sixteen-year-old blonde who trails after me is Zola's reclusive daughter, Magdalena. When the blonde closes the door, my first paranoid thought is I shouldn't be alone with her.

It's a trap.

She plops her agile form on the worn love seat in the corner of my living room. She acts bouncy like the puppy I had to give up when I came aboard.

"You should deputize me as your private detective," she says with a gleam in her eye that has me curious.

"Shouldn't you be home with your mom?"

"She's too busy hopping into bed with Jen."

Magdalena doesn't need this and I certainly don't need to know my two Senior Engineers are shacking up.

"I'm sorry," I say. "Do you have something to tell me?"

She hops up and examines a picture on the end table of me and my dad before he died. "Swear me in as your private detective and I'll help you catch the saboteur. Did I say that right?"

I nod. "You're too young. Your mother would never approve."

"That's why we need a secret ceremony."

She has my attention. I won't ask her to do anything risky, so I play along. "Raise your right hand and repeat after me. I, Magdalena Cohen swear to obey all orders given to me by Nina Rekovic as Chief of Security."

She so swears.

"So what's on your mind?"

"I know you're sympathetic to Returners even though you rounded them up. Well, I'm a Returner. Whew, I've never told anyone before, except Mom."

"You shouldn't be telling me."

"But you just deputized me."

I want to slap my head. *Keep playing along.* "Okay."

"The other girls ignore me 'cause I'm quiet, but I see everything." She plops back on the love seat, but she's too restless. "Returners didn't break into the fertility lab."

"You have evidence?"

"I just know."

"That's not good enough," I say. "You want something to drink?" I pour myself a Dream Drifter to help me forget about Carmen and fall into a deep slumber.

"Mom says I'm too young for that. I tried it once. It doesn't work for me."

I push the glass aside. "You shouldn't be—" I catch myself. I'm not her mom and she should be going. I nudge her toward the door.

Magdalena stops me before I open the door. "You shouldn't drink that junk, either. It can mess up your mind. I'll keep my eyes open for you."

"Don't get into trouble."

"Thanks. Give me a signal and I'll be there for you." She gives me a hug; then rushes out.

I return to my Dream Drifter and stare at the pale blue liquid. I've been relying too much on this. Has it dulled my senses?

* * *

Nina Rekovic Private Log 2098-10-19/8:33 AM

Carmen didn't come home again last night. When I reach the orange com-room on my morning rounds, she's gone. I do Eye-Pad scans of common areas; see more clusters, more whispering about Earth and sabotage. What I don't see are any officers. I check the engineering unit, and can't find Zola. *That's odd.*

Checking past cam history, I see why. All department heads except me have assembled in the captain's conference room. Zola is there in my absence. I check my wrist-com for missed communications. No messages except a cryptic: Eye C 26-Com. *Another crank note?*

I reach the conference room as the door slides open. Department heads rush past me like I'm invisible. I stop Zola. "Why wasn't I invited?" I whisper.

"Talk to the captain."

I enter the conference room to find Captain Beluga and

Carmen whispering in the corner. I strain to hear; they stop.

"Close the door," the captain says, which triggers the door to shut by itself.

"Why wasn't I invited?" I ask. "And don't say because I was asleep."

"Always direct. Very well, I've gotten reports that you sympathize with Returners."

"What evidence?" I ask.

"Confidential sources."

"As the ship's peace officer, I get people to talk instead of letting frustrations simmer. That's all."

Beluga approaches me. "This is a serious threat. I have to ask you to step down as Chief of Security."

"You use me to round up Returners, and then strip me of the title."

"I am removing you from security entirely. Carmen will take your place."

"I'm still Chief Engineer," I say, "unless you're taking that as well."

"Evidence points to three Returners sabotaging our fertility lab. Until I complete my investigation, I don't want you involved. You'll confine yourself to Engineering until further notice."

"Does that mean you're releasing the other Returners?"

"Not until things settle down."

I know Carmen turned the captain against me, but confronting her won't help. All I can do is stew as I leave the conference room. Unable to face my engineering duties, I head to the commons, wondering what evidence Captain Beluga could have. I know she tracks my movements. I don't think I said anything compromising.

Then I recall Magdalena.

I check last night's cam footage of the hallway outside my apartment. Carmen carries a suitcase from our apartment to the captain's quarters. Shaking, I clench my fists.

Carmen and Beluga?

I force myself to breathe, and detour away from the commons. Last thing I need is to run into anyone. Using my Eye-Pad, I find clear lifts and corridors back toward my apartment to freshen up. Returning to last night's cam recordings, I fast forward to when I came home.

Watching myself stroll toward the apartment, I wait for the moment Magdalena jumped out of the shadows. I reached the door. It opened. I went in. No Magdalena.

Was she already in the apartment? Having traced from when Carmen left to when I got home heightens my anxiety. Did Carmen let her in? Is Magdalena part of this? Her mom was at the meeting.

When I reach the apartment, I go in, expecting Magdalena to leap out again. She doesn't. I go the fridge for something to drink and find the glass of Dream Drifter where I placed it. It's black with writhing threads, parasites.

Magdalena?

I wish I had cam footage of last night inside the apartment. To the best of my knowledge that doesn't exist. Staring at the drink, I can almost feel those filaments entering my brain, leading to madness. I've seen its effects. Then I recall Magdalena telling me not to drink. Was she warning me? Did she know?

I check the message again: Eye C 26-Com. Of course, Icy is a nickname people gave me when I joined Maiden's Ark. I wasn't outgoing like Carmen. I kept to myself like Magdalena does.

On my Eye-Pad I check the commons on deck twenty-six, and find clusters of women gossiping. I listen in and hear concerns about our rumors. I check the timestamp for the message and scan cam history. Sergeant Yost was up from lockup talking with Senior Engineer Zola Cohen, Magdalena's mom. Ordinarily I wouldn't give it another thought. I listen and have to run the sound track through filters to make sense of the whispering.

"I've had no sympathy for Returners until now," Zola says. "I'm concerned about Earth survivors as well. But I don't want to lose my daughter over this."

"Can you get a message to the counsel?" Yost asks.

"I'll try."

"We need a ship-wide vote. Let the people decide."

"Captain won't allow it. She called a meeting this morning to remove Nina from security and the investigation."

The two women slipped away, just another gossip corner on the ship. How many others are sympathetic yet afraid to speak out?

It's time to choose sides, but either way, I betray people I care about. I don't want to turn this into a conflict where everyone loses. I have friends on both sides. At least I thought I did. This could become as contentious as when we embarked on this voyage against government and public protests.

I check my face. It looks like I haven't slept in weeks. Shrugging, I make my way back to the captain's office. On the way, I go to erase the Eye C message. I can't find it. I return to the video of Zola and Yost, and find the commons empty with the time-stamp of when they were there. I even see a plate on a nearby table that was there, but no Zola or Yost.

Did I imagine that?

It's probably a trap, but I enter the captain's office anyway. She already suspects me of being a Returner, might as well take a stand.

"I've been expecting you." Captain Beluga's big frame towers over me. "Sit."

I pace instead. "I don't believe I've ever given you cause to question my loyalty."

"Just being cautious."

"I gather Carmen is with you now."

The captain sits behind her large mahogany desk, something she brought from her corporate offices on Earth. "What was it you were saying about loyalty?"

"Mine is to you and everyone on the Maiden's Ark."

"I'm confused. You keep changing subjects."

Confused, yes. Changing subjects, no.

"You and Carmen betrayed my trust by hooking up. I can accept that. What I can't accept is pushing our small community into civil war."

Captain Beluga's eyes narrow. "What are you getting at?"

"You had me imprison those Returners who were outspoken before we heard about Earth. There are many more now."

"Give me names. We'll deal with them."

"I'm no longer in security, remember. Besides, I have reason to believe after hearing about Earth that the majority of the passengers and crew want to return."

That blow seems to hit the captain hard, but she recovers. "We're not turning around."

"I support your mission, Captain, but I think for the sake of peace, that we should put this to a vote. Let both sides make their case and let the majority decide."

"This is not a democracy."

"I know, Captain. I seek to avoid conflict that will tear us apart."

"Giving Returners a forum will do exactly that. This conversation is over."

* * *

Nina Rekovic Private Log 2098-10-19/1:42 PM

Unable to concentrate on my engineering duties, I drop down to Deck A to visit Francesca. Sergeant Yost won't let me enter the gray corridor leading to the jail cells. I'm tempted to bring up her meeting with Zola, but I don't want to out them.

Agitated, I return to engineering. I haven't seen Zola since she left the captain's meeting. She's probably running my investigation now. Instead, I find round-faced Senior Engineer Jen Adams, Zola's new lover. She's also one of Beluga's faithful, but I'm not sure where else to turn.

"Let's say, hypothetically, that we wanted to do a ship-wide vote, how could we do that?"

Her dark, tanned face is a mask, even as her eyes tighten, studying me. "Don't pull me into one of your schemes."

"When have I ever asked you to do anything that wasn't in the best interests of the crew and passengers?"

Jen starts counting off on her fingers, but says nothing.

"That's what I thought. Now humor me."

"I'll have to report this to the captain," Jen says.

"Report what? That I've asked you a hypothetical question?"

"You're up to something. Okay, assuming you alert everyone, they can respond giving their DNA prints on their wrist-coms. But returning will jeopardize our goals."

"Why not let the people decide?" I ask.

"I can't do that without captain's approval. She won't give it."

My Eye-Pad shows four newly deputized guards in uniform heading for engineering, for me. And they can track me.

"Jen, let me put this to the passengers. I promise to abide by their decision either way."

"I'm sorry, Chief. I can't."

"Then cover for me."

I hurry out of engineering, heading away from the four deputized guards. I don't fancy joining the other Returners on Deck A. I track the guards. While figuring where to go, I notice something strange on my Eye-com. It shows Magdalena walking next to me. But when I look around, I'm alone. The image disappears.

How did you do that?

Taking the lift up a deck, I move toward the commons lifts. I follow a faint line on the Eye-Pad that's not on the actual yellow nano-polymer floors. When I look for the guards, they're running around the engineering deck, bumping into each other. They've lost my signal.

Well, my deputized assistant, if this is your doing, I guess I owe you. I expect to take the lift to level twenty-six commons, but instead find myself on level eight, heading for Crazy Eights. It's the last place I want to go, especially when I find Carmen slumped at the bar.

I stand next to her and look at her ratty, shoulder-length brown hair. Horrible hair day. "Your back-stabbing might win you points with the captain, but everyone else should know what you are."

Carmen stands to confront me, but she's had too much Sedate Living to muster anger. *Feeling guilty, are you?*

I've never seen Carmen this wasted and wonder if Beluga pressured her to cheat on me. I push her back into her seat. "I don't want you back when this is over." I feel sorry for her when she slumps into her seat. Her eyes look up, pleading.

On my Eye-Pad, I see guards regroup and head for the lift. It didn't take long for someone to rat me out. The redhead, Delilah, stands by the door tapping on her E-Notepad. I grab the unit and drop it onto a yellow table, too bright for a bar.

I stand back in case she gets physical. "Why don't you and I air our grievances before whoever will listen. After all, we're too small a community to let this conflict simmer." I hope my deputized assistant can get this onto the intercom feed. I hear an echo from the blue corridor outside. The doors close.

Clever girl.

"I challenge you to debate here and now whether we should return to Earth and help survivors rebuild or continue along our way."

"You're nuts," the redhead says. "There's nothing to debate. We're not turning back."

"You're afraid?"

"You're on." The redhead stands aside so she can face her audience in the bar. "Everyone on this ship signed a contract to follow the captain and abide by her charter to start a new civilization. Everyone knew there was no going back. Yet, Returner-traitors had second thoughts. Too bad."

"That was before we got bad news about Earth," I say.

"Doesn't matter. Returning wastes valuable fuel and resources that will jeopardize our future. For what? A few thousand men on the moon base. Boo-hoo. We've sacrificed too much to get this far. Our future is forward, not back. We can't waste our prospects because they squandered theirs."

"We can't hold them accountable for this natural disaster."

"Maybe not," Delilah says, picking up her E-Notepad. "But if we turn back now, it'll take over five years to return. Chances of finding survivors is nil, none. Then we'd have wasted time and resources for nothing. It's triage. We have a better chance without them. Besides, from the beginning of time men have oppressed us. I will not give them another chance."

"You're afraid we'll have to bring them with us."

"Exactly. They'll never be able to sustain a civilization on the moon without Earth."

"Yet, we have for five years and expect to for generations." I check my Eye-Pad. Guards have reached the blue corridor outside Crazy Eights. They can't open the doors. *Thanks, special assistant.*

"Only if we don't squander what we have," Delilah says.

"All you say is true. It's not without risks."

Delilah grins. "Then you concede the debate."

"I would have before we learned that two asteroids collided into Earth." I say this to clear up rumors. "It's like what wiped out the dinosaurs. Only the moon base and asteroid miners have survived. They need our help."

"None of that changes the facts," Delilah says.

"The covenant and all decisions we've agreed to up until now were before we got this news. Our ship is the last hope of humans, here and back there."

"So let's create our new civilization, based on new values."

"If we don't return," I say. "We doom everyone left back home. The lunar base can't survive without resupply. We don't have to bring them onto the Ark. We can help them become self-sufficient. Then we can continue our mission knowing we've done our best."

"We'd lose over ten years for a lost cause."

"There's another reason to go back. I believe we can fix our EggFusion process. However, should the delicate system fail in future, we doom humankind by not leaving an alternative."

"We need to make sure it doesn't fail by keeping Returners away from it," Delilah says. "You've offered nothing convincing."

"Then try this. Returning is the compassionate alternative, the moral choice, the best chance for the survival of the human race. We value compassion. Yet when called, we turn our backs. Our new civilization is built on principles of helping fellow humans. If we fail now, then we give lie to principles that inspired us on this journey. All arguments against return given this new information are based on selfish considerations."

My Eye-Pad shows the guards have brought Jen to help pry open the door to Crazy Eights.

"I call upon all crew and passengers on the Maiden's Ark. Vote your conscience. Let the captain know where you stand. I'll abide by the will of the people."

"Bold words," Delilah says. "But you're going to jail. Hope you enjoy cleaning recycling tanks."

The captain joins the guards and Jen trying to force the door.

"I cast my vote for return," I say. "Everyone please cast yours. Then abide by the results. We cannot continue to fight among ourselves and expect our new society to flourish."

"Oh, shut up." Carmen pushes me away from Delilah's E-Notepad. "What's all this fuss?"

I grab the E-Notepad. "I've had enough of you. You betrayed me by sleeping with the Captain and turning on me like a rabid dog. That's not how you treat your partner."

Zola arrives outside and gets the door open. Six deputized guards in uniform rush in followed by the captain, who towers over them.

"Arrest her," Beluga says.

"You might want to look at the results first." I hold up Delilah's E-Notepad. "Eighty percent in favor of return, with over forty percent voting."

"Numbers mean nothing," the captain says.

"They mean people are upset and you're not listening. In fact I now have evidence that you sabotaged the fertility lab so you could blame Returners before they could lobby for return."

The captain turns to Zola. "Turn off the loudspeaker."

Zola shakes her head. "I stand with the people, Captain. Did you sabotage the lab?"

"All lies." Captain McDaniels turns to the guards. "Arrest them both, for sedition."

"Are you sure you want to imprison eighty percent of the passengers and crew? That's not what we signed up for."

When the guards hesitate, the captain turns to Sergeant Tucker. "I promote you to Chief of Security. Arrest these two and anyone who acts treasonous."

Sergeant Tucker clears her throat. "Then I place you under arrest for sabotaging the fertility lab and trumping up charges to arrest Returners."

"You can't arrest me," Captain McDaniels says. "This is my ship."

"You just gave me the authority to arrest traitors."

* * *

Nina Rekovic Private Log 2098-10-19/2:49 PM

As new Chief of Security, Tucker releases the Returners from their cells on Deck A and adds two new occupants, Captain McDaniels and Senior Engineer Jen Adams. By popular acclaim and experience, the executive officers name Delilah Witherspoon to captain the ship during the trip back, despite her resistance to going back. Francesca returns to managing our meals.

Slowing, turning around, and speeding toward Earth takes over a month, but when the final results of the second poll come back, over ninety-five percent of the crew and passengers agree it's the right thing to do.

While I avoid Crazy Eights, I see Carmen from time to time. She begs me to take her back and forgive her for bending to Beluga's will. I might have considered how she fell under our captain's power, but I can't forgive those tiny black worms in my Dream Drifter. I send that through hazmat disposal. Based on the evidence, Carmen joins the captain in a separate cell on Deck A.

It takes a month, but Zola gets the fertility lab working. It would have taken longer, but she pours her own betrayal at the hands of her lover, Jen, into fixing what Jen destroyed.

That leaves Magdalena without parental supervision. While I look after her, she teaches me the fine points of 3D chess and helps me get through Carmen's betrayal.

One thing still troubles me. "How did you know my drink was contaminated?"

Magdalena grins. "People think I'm slow because I don't talk much. The captain gave Carmen something that she held at arm's length like poison. Yet, she brought it home."

"I owe you many thanks. We all do."

"I'm scared about going back." Magdalena looks down.

"Then why—"

"I hated Jen so much I thought going back would make things better. It won't, will it?"

I shake my head. "No, but we'll manage."

■ ■ ■

WATCHING YOU

(Big brother watching; man who can't resist)

Harold Winters is fearful when he gets up in the morning and when he goes to bed at night, on his way to work and coming home, and certainly at work. He fears threats he sees on his home vid and those the Standards Board pays him to watch at work. Like other citizens, he puts his trust in Phase V of the Patriot Act, inaugurated after yet another failed terrorist attack.

Sitting in his Patriot Blue cube, third row, fourth down, at the Federal Civil Standards Board, Chicago Office, Harold keeps his eyes on his 42-inch screen lest he miss another imminent threat. Onscreen are nine live views displayed by Art-Intel, the controller supplied by Livermore International Network Corporation (LINC). *Omnipresent INC*, Harold says only to himself. He strains to remember a time before LINC replaced the Internet/web so it could record and sift trillions of vid and voice feeds from all across America.

As a Patriot Blue, Harold is a bona fide second-class citizen with no choice of jobs. He settles for what is offered: playing second fiddle to an artificial intelligence. The last time he saw his parents, they begged him not to resist as they had. Instead, he should adapt to a society that requires all citizens to have RFID implants. When his parents fled, the Standards Board reclassified them to Underclass Red and then Outcast Gray.

Harold couldn't attend their funerals because Outcast Grays and Patriot Blues can't mingle. Of course, Blues know they can't aspire to Privileged Green or, LINC forbid, Honorable Purple, except for Cora Thompson. She is the sweet honey-haired woman on his screen acting in a Board-approved morality sitcom. Though she was born Patriot Blue, the Board upgraded her to Privileged Green so she could act.

Harold's chair vibrates. "Back to work!" The artificial voice carries the unmistakable bass of his boss, Mel Gardner. Someone chuckles nearby. Harold cannot see who it is over the partitions.

Convinced that Art-Intel could do his job, he glances up to look for cams, but of course, they are microscopic. He scans the row of blue plastic plants he suspects serve to hide cams he hasn't yet found.

Returning his attention to the screen, Harold zooms in on one of his nine views. *Have to remain vigilant for terrorist threats.* He is amazed at how Art-Intel culls through so much data, linking searches, purchases, and personal connections to tag someone as a threat. He likes to trace backward to figure out how the clues fit, and what Art-Intel saw that he didn't. Mel ridicules him for being inferior to a biochip.

Onscreen, a dark-haired Patriot Blue woman hardly seems a threat. She sends a cute redheaded girl into the scan-chamber entry for Kerr-Mart, a universal store accessible to Patriot Blues. The girl enters the store. Thick Plexiglas doors lock, trapping the woman inside the chamber.

"Access denied!"

Splitting screens, Harold pulls up her file. There it is—she had an abortion. How could she be so wicked to deny her sweet child life? Harold shakes his head. *That must be a mistake.* The child is there, frightened, staring at her mom.

"Your status is downgraded to Underclass Red," an artificial voice tells the woman.

A brown-shirt escorts her daughter away. Harold pulls the child's file. A Privileged Green couple wants to adopt this redhead, but the mother refuses to give up her only child. This will open doors for the child like when they upgraded Cora. *Good for you.*

The dark-haired woman pounds on the Plexiglas barrier keeping her from her retreating child. Harold wishes he could tell her the good news. When the redhead tries to run to her mom, the brown-clothed guard picks her up and carries her down a long corridor to a waiting van. The woman's anguish tugs at Harold. Not only is she losing her daughter, she will lose her apartment and her credit. Only menial jobs will be open to her.

When the scan-chamber opens from outside, brown-shirts sedate the woman and haul her away. Aware that cams are watching him, Harold copies the feed for the evening news so everyone can see. Sanctity of life forbids abortion. Penalties are steep. At least the daughter won't suffer for her mother's crime. Harold isn't convinced.

The next feed shows an Outcast Gray, his scruffy blond beard and tattered gray trench coat hallmarks of non-citizens, who are denied society's benefits. The Board prohibits prostitutes, druggies, murderers, rapists, and other dregs from the Metropolitan domain. Yet here he is in the Loop. Harold shivers. A troop of brown-shirts surrounds the outcast. An Underclass Red woman tries to help him down an alley. She risks a downgrade to Outcast Gray. *Is this love?* Harold wonders.

Brown-shirts shoot the man in the head. The woman goes to her friend, but he is dead. His implant registers no heart or brain activity. As required by law, the patrol has neutralized the terror threat. Each color can downgrade except Outcast Gray. For them, the next step is an overcrowded prison or death. Brown-shirts did him a favor. The Board downgrades the woman to Outcast Gray. Harold tags another story for evening news feeds, further justification for the new security rules.

All day Harold scans for news, keeping one view on honey-haired Cora and another on the woman who watched her boyfriend die. She should have known that mixed relationships are illegal. He pulls up her file. Several months ago, with Harold's help, the Board downgraded her to Red for associating with an underclass. She welcomed that change until the Board reclassified the man she was with to Outcast Gray. It is easy to move down, almost impossible to move up, unless you are beautiful like honey-haired Cora.

Justice is swift. Brown-shirts take the newly Outcast Gray woman by jet-chopper beyond Metro. From a height of ten feet, they push her out. She lands in swampy wetlands. She struggles to her feet, curses and makes odd hand gestures. Harold's screen doesn't translate, but he remembers his parents using them before they vanished.

Curious, Harold finds a picture of the woman's earlier

boyfriend and compares it to the dead man. He finds the similarities as shocking as the differences. It is eerie how downgrading can change a man. The broken nose and sad eyes match, despite the haggard weathered look of what seems like a much older man. Harold adds her earlier transgression to the news as further validation for her adjustment. Harold congratulates himself on his knack for story. Yet he can't help wondering what possessed this woman twice to risk everything. *Is this romantic love?* He shudders at what sacrifices she made.

The next feed is trickier. A Patriot Blue man comes into money, too much says Art-Intel. Lists of transactions pour over Harold's screen, no large sums, but they look suspicious. He doesn't find anything unusual until he thinks of his own spending. Where is the food bill? There are no food charges for months. *Neat trick.*

Scanning back Harold finds where the man previously shopped and looks for unusual activity. He is proud of his ability to track credits forward and back like solving math puzzles. When he hits a dead-end, Harold finds the man on cam and lifts the ID embedded in his silk shirt, something Blues can't afford. Sure enough, a Green woman purchased it with credit from Senator Maverick Lacey. *Got you,* Harold thinks, though it is risky going after an Honorable Purple.

"Harold, my man." A heavy hand presses his shoulder.

A burly African-American, Mel Gardner is Privileged Green, Harold's boss, and director of the Chicago facility. Once a month Mel invites Harold to dinner; picks him up in his vintage Majestic, a Green-approved model. Over steak, Harold endures Mel's complaints about trying to scrape by on a Privileged Green income. Harold can only dream.

Mel practically lifts Harold from his seat, removes Harold's earpiece, and clasps his hand. "You've been selected employee of the month. What do you say?"

Harold is speechless. This is his first. Will it mean a bonus? He has heard of such, though never for a Patriot Blue.

Releasing the handshake, Mel marches off without inviting Harold back to his office. The interruption is brief, leaving Harold feeling special and confused.

When he sits down, the Lacey file is gone. His eyes moisten; he is employee of the month. Has he outperformed coworkers? He wants to compare notes, to talk to someone other than Mel, but his boss forbids him from discussing his work even with coworkers. *You can't tell who might be a traitor,* Mel once said as Harold signed a thick confidentiality agreement in legalese he couldn't begin to understand. He has no one to share his good fortune with.

I am all alone.

Harold pulls up feeds from his apartment and fills all nine views. His home is a Patriot Blue cube like that of his coworkers. He watches their places now and then and is certain they watch his. Rooms are identical down to pale blue décor. If he mistakenly walked into the wrong apartment, he would feel right at home.

His Patriot Blue appliances include micro-cooker, wash/dry unit, and fridge. He has a wall vid with LINC, but only Blue-approved channels: three cooking, two gardening, and eight spiritual that all sound alike. He can watch sitcoms ending with infraction adjustments, news vids, and self-improvement feeds intended to mold him into a model citizen. He has no interest, but they are friends to keep him company at night.

The Privileged Green condos he has seen have a second bedroom, although he can't imagine how he would use it. Appliances are bigger, newer, and more diverse. Green vid LINC accesses more shows. Sometimes he monitors them from work to see what he is missing. Greens can watch wealth-building programs, but nothing that show Harold how he could move up from Patriot Blue.

At least he is not Red. They get efficiency lofts, barely big enough for a bed, cooker, and stacked laundry. Yet even that is better than living on the streets, or being an Outcast Gray. Maybe that woman's dismal prospects are what drove her to help her boyfriend.

Harold pulls up Cora's sitcom and grins. She looks pretty in her lively green floral dress. Before his boss catches him, he changes feeds to the streets and rail station. The monorail loads the last of an early shift of Blues so they can return to their empty apartments. Like him, they micro-cook prepackaged meals, and consume their daily quota of drinks. Then, they sit before the vid for conditioning before another day of work. Harold's shift ends. He doesn't want to be late.

* * *

Grabbing his coat, Harold rushes down three flights of stairs to avoid having to wait for the crowded elevators. In the lobby, he falls in line behind coworkers dressed in a dozen shades of blue to mark their class as they emerge from work. *You don't want anyone mistaking you for Privileged Green, like that could happen.* He doesn't need his coat since he can travel indoors from the office to the monorail and on to his apartment, but someone attacked the monorail last year. To get home, he had to walk five blocks in the cold.

He hurries down the corridor toward the monorail ramps, keeping a watchful eye on brown-shirt guards. *Never draw attention if you don't have to.* When he reaches the turnstile, he sees ahead of him that bun of honey-hair and the sleek shape of Cora's green floral dress. A moment sooner and he might have gathered a whiff of her sweet perfume and risked a hello. She turns with a dreamy smile and boards the Green compartment where he won't be welcome.

Do you recognize me?

He can't share this feeling of belonging with her because he has no hope of that ever happening. He wants no trouble, only to glimpse her and see her safely home. *That is enough,* he tells himself. *Remember, thoughts only remain private when kept to myself.* Yet, memory fades. *If I don't record or share my thoughts, how can I trust they won't disappear?* You can't speak or write without the Standards Board recording everything, so how can you have private thoughts?

His father warned him about the end of privacy, but it didn't seem important at the time. Now that Harold's private thoughts are about Cora, he desperately wants to yell them from the roof terrace, or at least write them on a notepad he hid when the government banned paper. They want to discourage secret messages. Of course, writing anything off the LINC brings adjustments. Mostly, Harold wants to share his thoughts with Cora because of the connection he feels, even though they have only exchanged polite glances.

For two months, since she started acting on her sitcom, Harold has watched the azure-eyed honey-blonde at work and at the monorail. He feels like Romeo wooing Juliet, for she is Privileged Green and he is lowly Blue. He not only doesn't have a chance, any interaction is strictly "verboten." Yet, she has been more pleasant to him than any of his fellow Blues. Like him, they keep their heads down and struggle to get by. He can't stop thinking about her. That is his one private thought, something the state doesn't yet own.

* * *

Harold reaches his desk early the next morning to research Cora. The Standards Board has slated her to become wife to an Honorable Purple, one of several wives, no doubt, since she is Green and the Board permits Purples to have multiple wives like the Biblical patriarchs. She deserves better.

Keeping one of his views on Cora, Harold feels connected, as he hasn't since losing his parents. Back before the Standards Board, he could have approached her and imagined a better life. He longs for those golden days, and imagines his parents would approve of Cora as a daughter-in-law. After all, she is a model, not the naked outcast type, but a model citizen, an exemplar.

Cora's file shows her Patriot Blue parents left her with a Privileged Green family so she could move up. Yet, she is lonely, like Harold. He pulls up history feeds of Cora in her apartment. She cries at her bathroom mirror with water gushing. She must think that drowns out her words: "Mom, Dad, I miss you so much. Why can't I see you?" Why? Because Blues and Greens can't mingle, except under Board-approved conditions like work or at the monorail.

It is at the mirror with water running that Cora shares private thoughts, fears and expectations. She suspects an arranged marriage, which she doesn't want. She longs for someone and as Privileged Green, she is permitted to choose from among other Greens. Yet she keeps to herself. Harold sheds a tear like when his parents left. He hungers for family, but as Patriot Blue, Harold has to wait until the Board chooses for him.

For LINC's sake, they have it wrong. Cora is meant for me. Are you waiting for me to act? If I don't, will I lose you forever?

Daring not to enlarge her image, Harold contents himself with a six-inch screen of her in her dressing room, tablet-writing sitcom notes and rehearsing for her performance. Through the vid-feed, her life unfolds like a movie. She seems so close he could touch her. This is dangerous, but he can't help himself.

Envying the men she performs with, Harold denies her access to leave her dressing room for a moment so he can imprint her image. She looks annoyed, but not angry. Though LINC delays are common, he apologizes in his private thoughts. It is like having to wait longer for the elevator or monorail, one of life's little nuisances. Yet he is touching her, even if only in a manipulative way. He digs his fingernail into his palm. *This is wrong. I have to stop.*

He scans through live city views, sees nothing of interest, and flips back to review her file. Cora struggles more than most Greens. As an entertainer, she hungers for clothes and adornments she can't afford. Harold knows the desire for what you can't have, the burning passion that can be used against you if, LINC forbid, they find you out.

When he returns to Cora's active feed, she isn't in her dressing room or on the set. He locates her leaving by the back door. She looks distraught. He pulls a second feed from across the street and zooms in on her face. Her eyes fill with tears. A history feed shows that moments earlier she received a message that her mother died. She can't attend the funeral since she can't mingle with Blues. A fourth view shows her father at the funeral alone. *Bastards.*

Back on the street, Harold watches three Underclass Reds with scruffy beards. They approach Cora. It isn't safe; she is distracted, not paying attention. Harold sets off an alarm at a nearby jewelry store. That startles the Reds and alerts her. He opens a door for her to a Purple clothier. The Standards Board forbids Greens from this store, but seeing the men, she enters the scan-chamber. She is shaking, terrified. One of the men tries the door. Harold seals it. Brown-shirts pull up in a truck. One Red stumbles and falls against the wall. Blood splatters the back of his shirt. His companions flee. Brown-shirts carry the injured man to the truck.

Harold has no doubt where they will dump him.

Cora looks up toward the camera, forces a smile, and mouths: *thank-you.* She is talking to him. He saved her and she understands. When he releases the door to the street, she leaves, holding her head up as if nothing happened.

"Loitering again?" Mel hangs overhead like a dark cloud.

Harold scrambles the feeds, and lets Art-Intel select his nine views.

Mel blocks the screen. "Dreaming is for fools."

"I wasn't."

Harold scoots back to see his boss' face, but Mel retreats to his office. Harold follows. He tries to figure out how he can challenge what LINC records. He is spending too much time on Cora. He expects another lecture about terror threats and the need for him to focus.

Mel closes the door to his greenly accented office. "You've

done your nation a great service." He sits Harold down and stands over him. "But you grow too attached. Wanting what you can't have brings misery. Accept your lot. Let it bring you happiness."

Harold nods. *I should.*

"She does appeal to the eye, doesn't she? I was thinking of approaching her." Mel stares down at Harold, looking for betrayal of private thoughts.

Harold buries his thoughts deeper, but his stomach knots at the thought of his boss approaching Cora when he can't.

"Good. I like you, Harold. You could have a very long career here. We do vital work. Can you imagine if colors mixed? No, you were too young. We had social strife and terror. No one was safe. It's best that people accept their lot and remove temptations."

Harold plasters a smile on his face as Mel continues, "Remember, Harold, there are no victimless crimes."

What about that Underclass Red woman giving up everything to be with her man, Harold wanted to ask. *She wasn't hurting anyone.*

"You hear me, Harold? That's why we no longer have lawyers. They create conflict and unhappiness. You don't remember, but I do."

Maybe the cute redhead's mom didn't have an abortion. Maybe someone, like Harold, got bored and wrote her up. Did that Privileged Green couple pay to alter her records so they could take her child? What if rules are arbitrary? What if there are victimless crimes?

Harold begins shaking and falls from his chair.

"Are you okay?" Mel asks, looking concerned.

"I see the light. I know the true path."

Mel helps Harold up. "See, all you needed was an attitude adjustment."

* * *

Ever since he first spotted Cora's honey-hair at the monorail station and received a faint smile in response, Harold conjured ways to approach her. What should he say? How would she react? It would be tricky. Despite listening to her before her mirror, he can't be sure he has all her private thoughts. Then there are ever-present cams. He calls up monorail feeds looking for gaps.

After work, while he waits for the turnstile to accept his implant's signal, Harold fears ending up like that woman who lost her daughter. Then he sees that glow of honey-hair ahead of him.

He tries to recall where he found the cams. His brain scrambles with anticipation. He closes his eyes; slows his breathing. Elevated heart rate can cause turnstiles to reject. When the light flashes green, he surges forward.

Harold remembers the cam locations he scanned this morning, but he can't be sure he has found them all. At work, when he found gaps, Art-Intel brought new feeds that weren't there before. As he hurries up the platform, he hears the whir of the monorail. He keeps Cora in the fuzzy edges of his vision so the cams won't pick up that he's following her.

Long sleek cylinders glide into the station, the first Green, several Blue, and aft a small Red compartment. Despite a heated platform, Harold draws his dark overcoat around his collar so that only the bottoms of his trousers show blue. He heads for the first Blue car, which is already filling up. That is the way of life. Blues have crowded compartments, Greens ample space, and Reds pack in like toothpicks, pushing and shoving as befits their class.

Cora lets a pregnant woman and her male companion get into the Green car before her. Harold reaches the first Blue car. Commuters jostle for limited seats. He is ten feet from Cora. She turns, smiles, and disappears inside the Green compartment.

Harold follows her. He recalls a cam gap inside the monorail doors, where he can have a private moment with Cora. He lunges at the opening, stumbles on the step, and falls face first into the aisle at her feet. He gazes up at her green floral dress.

Looking alarmed, she gets to her feet and helps him up. Her touch is firm, but friendly. Her face remains contorted. That is when Harold notices alarms pounding his ears. He forgot the door sensors would reject his implant. He violated the sanctity of Green space. He kisses her hand, a gesture he recalls his father doing with his mom.

Cora pushes him off the train and returns to her seat. Her face carries a dozen messages but mostly fear. Greens scramble off the platform. Shouting, Blues hurry away, abandoning the nearby monorail door. He is a terrorist, having struck terror into the lives of law-abiding citizens. *What have I done?*

A husky brown-shirt runs toward him. Knowing his adjustment will tear him farther from his beloved Cora, Harold runs toward the turnstiles. The Board will downgrade him for sure to Underclass Red; strip him of his job, his apartment, his meager pay.

They will make him a desk clerk at the reeducation center, or put him in for reeducation. He would take anything but interrogation where they would dig at his private thoughts.

Angry voices pelt him from behind. How can he be so rude, so Blue? Knowing turnstiles will reject him, Harold leaps over, ripping his overcoat on the metal bridge. Pushing through the bewildered crowd trying to get to the platform, he races downstairs. He breaks out onto the nearly empty boulevard. Red dregs scurry about, cleaning the streets. Harold runs as hard as he can. Cold wind slaps his face. He feels alive. His heart thumps in his chest. He can only imagine the medical stream his implant is providing. He remembers the Outcast Gray man trying to escape and getting shot. *Bad plan.*

Sirens approach. There is no escape. Harold is on every surveillance feed. Dozens like him back at the office will follow his movements, check his history, and measure his heart rate and brain waves. *Why did I do this? One smile from that angelic face and I ruined my life. What about Cora? Will they adjust you for my recklessness? What will you tell them when they interrogate you?*

He wants to reach her to tell her how sorry he is. He aches to keep them from hurting her. But they will track him through his implant, wherever he goes. Instinct sets in, self-preservation. Seeing brown-shirts, Harold darts into an alley where Reds cluster. Theirs is a desperate place for marginal lives. He has seen morality vids of Blues straying into Red neighborhoods. Harold is ready to collapse from fright, but isn't he about to join them?

Voices yell from behind. "Stop before your adjustment gets worse."

Harold runs. He believes he can get away, yet knows that he can't. How can he hold two divergent beliefs at the same time? This new sensation spurs him on. He is desperate, terrified, a terrorist. Yet what presses into his mind is Cora wanting a better life.

He trips or falls; maybe someone shoved him. He can't be sure. Instead of hitting the ground, he flies through a doorway. Moments blur with strange images—filth he has never seen except on vid. His nostrils pinch, trying to choke off the putrid stench of rotten food and garbage. Smoke burns his eyes. His skin feels as if covered in stinging ants. How can people live like this? He loses his footing; keeps moving, half running, half carried. Stairs lead down and down as if entering the underworld.

When he comes to a stop, bright lights blind him. A faceless, mud-haired woman breaks into view. Harold recalls the woman who tried to protect her companion. He is convinced it is the same couple he helped catch last year.

"Who are you? What do you want?"

* * *

Despite having seen adjustments on vid-feed, it still astounds Harold how quickly his status can change. One moment you are minding your own business, in a life you have adapted to. Then it is gone. You have no job, no credits. You lose your home. You can't show your face. You are a lost soul at the mercy of powers you cannot control. Beat down, you will do as they ask for to resist is pointless.

While Brown-shirts escort Harold to interrogation, he plays over in his mind all the lives he has watched change. He can't stop thinking of Cora. He has to see her.

Brown-shirts march him down a bland beige corridor he has never seen before. Lights become dimmer until he has to strain to see the stain-marked floor. They thrust him into a room bathed in light so bright he closes his eyes tight and sees black brightness.

After the door slams, Harold hears a familiar bass voice. "I warned you obsession would lead to despair."

Sweating, Harold stands on shaky legs. His eyes cannot adjust in a room bathed in white, as if every inch of wall, floor and ceiling radiates heat. He has no perspective as to whether the room is large or small. He cannot see Mel; can't tell if there is a table or chair. Harold shakes too much to bring himself to ask.

"I had high hopes for you, Harold. You do good work, but this obsession shames you. You see that, don't you?"

Harold nods. He likes easy questions that he can answer. He is glad he can't see his boss, yet feels that presence hover nearby, over his shoulder.

"Speak up! Say the words."

"I ... see." Harold squints, because he can't see. His knees want to buckle, but he dare not ask for a seat.

"You've not only shamed yourself, you've embarrassed me. You forced the Board to act on behalf of the woman. Observe the extent and repercussions of your crime."

Lights dim. The wall morphs into a room with a table and two chairs. Cora sits across from a gray-haired man, a Privileged Green

118

by his clothes. Harold approaches. As he crosses his chamber, the image shimmers and fades. His hand reaches for Cora. Realizing his mistake, he slaps it to his side.

The gray-hair says, "You know your crime, don't you?"

"The man tripped."

The gray-hair leans toward her. "He saved your life. Surely, you knew. You even thanked him. You've grown fond of him, haven't you?"

"How could I? We've never met."

Behind the gray-hair, the screen shows her acknowledging Harold's hello. "Come now, Cora. You know what happens if your reputation is tarnished? Have you thought about this man?"

"Absolutely not!" Looking terrified, she brushes honey hair from her face. The Board can downgrade her for not living up to the Green code of conduct. "He reminded me of my brother. I haven't seen him since—"

"Since you were elevated to Privileged Green." The gray-hair's face softens. "Lucky for you an Honorable Purple wants you as his wife. You'll gain status and can escape the Blues."

Her face turns sour. Harold gave the Board the leverage to force her into a marriage she doesn't want. If she gives herself to this Purple, all will be forgiven. But Green wives aren't accepted into Purple society, particularly those elevated from Blue. She will be isolated and miserable. That will be her adjustment and there is nothing Harold can do.

Cora nods somberly. "Can I meet him first?"

"I'm sure you know him. It's Senator Lacey." The gray-hair holds out his hand to close the deal.

She expected this, Harold knows from her mirror-talk, but there is no joy in her face. Maverick Lacey is married to a Purple. Cora will be no more than his mistress, one of many. Walking toward her image, Harold looks for an exit, as if breaking free he would know where to find her. She is too good for this. That is when he realizes she was elevated from Blue to Green for this very purpose. Anger surfaces, stiffening his quivering jaw. He tries to wash this away before his implant betrays him.

"Come now, Cora," the gray-hair says. "You've contaminated yourself by associating with a Blue. This great outcome is available because we caught things in time."

"I … I'll marry the senator."

"Good." Gray-hair grins his victory.

The image morphs to a small chapel. Time has passed. Cora stands with Senator Maverick Lacey, the womanizer. She looks angelic, innocent, frightened. Harold's knees buckle; he falls to the floor. He expects her to notice and come to his aid, but she isn't really here.

"You shame yourself," Mel's voice echoes. "You betray your deepest thoughts. You cannot hide them from me."

Lying on the floor, Harold watches Senator Lacey kiss the bride. It is a tiny wedding—the couple, gray-hair, and a preacher who looks like an old-style lawyer. Tears stream down Harold's cheeks as he watches Lacey escort his Cora away.

The image vanishes and light bathes the room again. Harold wipes his cheeks.

"You are fortunate," Mel's disembodied voice says. "She's gone as temptation. No more sitcom. You'll lose a month's credits, but I'll let you keep your job if you behave. You came close to losing everything. Don't disappoint me again."

"Bless you, oh privileged one," Harold mutters. "Bless you for your wisdom, benevolence, and for my modest adjustment."

Harold suppressed his private thoughts so deep he fears never retrieving them again, but they rattle around, like an energized ping-pong ball. *Damn the color-classes.* Cora won't be happy as a second or third wife, mistress really. Harold wonders if Mel knows he is thinking of setting her free, no matter what the risk.

■ ■ ■

REGINA SHEN: INTO THE STORM

(Prequel to Regina Shen series; incorporated into Regina Shen: Resilience)

Richmond Swamps, June ACM 296

A gray Department of Antiquities patrol boat motored across our path. I paddled into a cattail-covered cove, kept a wary eye for alligators, and waited for the gray-uniformed agents to leave. In the morning heat, sweat trickled down my neck and soaked my green canvas top, causing me to itch. I ignored the irritation and swarms of black flies.

"Regina, we should go home," Colleen whispered from the front of my log-boat.

"We'll be fine, sis," I said to keep her calm. "School is safe." I hoped.

While there was ebb and flow to life in the swamps, three patrol sightings so far this week were unusual, and it was only Thursday. Something was up.

When the Antiquities boat headed up the channel, we crossed and tied the mooring rope to reeds below our school. I made sure the log-boat was secure and hidden from view, in case the patrol returned. Then I led Colleen up the rocky incline beside stilts that kept the wood-frame buildings above water.

Colleen and I hurried to our respective classes. There was no one in the clearing between the buildings, on the stairs, or at the tiny balconies by classroom entrances. I ran up the steps, pushed

121

open the rickety wood door, and dropped my wet, muddy boots beside others on a stone slab inside.

School was the best part of my day. I didn't have to watch my twelve-year-old sister, since she was secure in her own classroom. Mo-Mere, our nickname for our teacher, Marisa Seville, brought the dozen girls in her class warm soup of beans, turtle, and spuds.

My favorite part: she let me touch real books—brittle paper ones, yellowed, edges worn, with stories that tickled my mind, stories the World Federation had purged from the Mesh-cloud. Mo-Mere's books made the six-days-a-week slog through miles of swamp in a hollowed-out log worthwhile.

"Regina," Mo-Mere placed her weathered face next to mine and whispered in a warm voice with a tough edge. "You might be my best student, but that doesn't excuse tardiness." She pinched my cheeks to let me know she meant both comments.

She was too kind. Though I was fifteen, doing seventeen-year-old work, I took too much of Mo-Mere's time. She was like a second mom to me. In fact, the other girls gossiped that she was my donor mother, providing half her DNA to Mom to conceive me in the local fertility clinic. Mom refused to talk to me of such matters.

Mo-Mere nudged me toward the four rows of four small tables facing the front of the room. "Take your seat. I was telling the class I received a report of a Category-5 hurricane bearing down on us tomorrow night."

I shrugged. This would be the second big storm of the year.

A new student sat in the first row, in front of Mo-Mere's rough-cut maple desk. I took the vacant seat next to her, where no one else wanted to sit, so I could learn without all the distractions of the older girls whispering. Mostly they gossiped about how I had a little girl's body. My hips hadn't filled out, and I refused to stuff my bra like two girls did.

We all wore the same faded green canvas trousers and pullovers. Raw canvas came in one color—dull green—and most of us Marginals had nothing to barter for expensive dyes.

"Let's pray to the Blessed Mary," Mo-Mere said, as part of our Federation-required morning ritual.

Tapping my foot, I mumbled along with the other students, paying no attention to words as distant as the world beyond the

Great Barrier Wall, a massive concrete structure that separated us from the Federation.

Our teacher pointed a gnarled wooden stick at the board on the right side of the room. "Let's recite our Twelve Commandments."

I mouthed by rote, "Thou shalt not kill," "Thou shalt not steal," "Thou shalt not leave the Marginal swamps without Federation permission." Blah, blah, blah.

"Who can tell Beth how the Federation began?" Mo-Mere's intense eyes looked from student to student. When no one volunteered, she looked at me to answer for the new student. Her sharp eyes drilled into me until I nodded.

While I longed to be out, making preparations for the storm, my heart raced to recall official histories. "Three centuries ago our atmosphere warmed, glaciers melted, and oceans rose, destroying croplands. The Great Collapse threatened civilization. The Community Movement rose up and established the World Federation to restore peace and save us." The last was a big lie. Their Federation and Department of Antiquities purged knowledge and books from Before the Community Movement (BCM) and eliminated anyone who threatened their control.

I stopped my foot from thumping on the creaky wood floor.

Mo-Mere looked around the classroom then at me. "Very good, Regina. The Federation built the Great Barrier Wall to our west to hold back the seas." She gave the same introduction to each new student. Listening to it again had me squirming in my seat.

"Why are we on the wet side of the Wall?" I blurted out, since Marginals had helped build the Wall centuries ago.

Mo-Mere scowled at such an obvious question. "Why don't you answer for Beth's benefit?"

I shifted my bony rump on the wood seat, hung my head, and gave the official answer. "Marginals were cast out after they rebelled." Except my ancestors had been in the Federation at that time.

"And?" Mo-Mere prompted.

"We must work hard to prove our worth to the Federation." I looked up. "But every year, the waters swamp more of our lands. Soon, we won't have anywhere to live."

"That's why you must work for a chance at university."

"But—"

"Regina Shen! That's enough. See me after class."

While pretending to frown in shame, inside I smiled at the chance to spend more time with Mo-Mere. Looking around, I realized I'd dug a bigger grave for myself with the other girls. I wanted to learn, even if they didn't.

Mo-Mere stood in front of her desk, towering over me. "This storm could be the worst in my lifetime." She let that sink in.

Worst was relative. Each storm took homes and land, and made us scramble, but they were all bad. She seemed more worried this time.

"Since the storm isn't expected until tomorrow night, school will be open in the morning, unless your moms want you home. Don't take unnecessary risks. If you do come, bring examples of how you've prepared. In order to survive, we must share with other students and neighbors."

She looked around the small room to be sure we were listening. "Find the highest shelter you can with protection against storm surges. Make sure you have emergency supplies, including medicines. Think how the storm will affect your gardens and how you'll hunt for food. Be careful what you scrounge to eat. Remember the pictures I showed you of poisonous seafood."

* * *

Detention for me meant Colleen had to stay at school until I was ready to take her home.

"I'm hungry," she whined when I came to tell her. "I want to go home." Her pleading eyes tore at me.

"Mom won't be there," I said. "She's diving salvage to barter for new boots." This was a stretch. I had no idea what Mom did while we were away.

Colleen stared at her toes. "Why do you have to get detention every day?"

"I'll make it up to you later."

I scooted her into her seat and hurried back to my classroom.

Mo-Mere lived in a one-room apartment attached to the classroom. She had a bed, a small clothes chest, and her kitchen nook. Stilts kept the buildings above surge waters—so far. But each storm brought the channel closer.

Her apartment gave off a hint of welcoming fragrances from her potpourri, a collection of hybrid herbs she bred and grew in a garden across the clearing. The floral scent masked the odor of rot and decay from ever-humid wood and fumes from hot tar on the roof. The calming scents contrasted with sharp, lush swamp odors each time I stepped outside.

Mo-Mere stood over a wood-burning stove in the corner brewing an herbal tea. "What am I to do with you?" She turned to face me. "Your mother wants you in school. Eleventh grade is as high as we go and you're beyond that." She raised my chin until I looked at her. "I'm not scolding. I've never had such a precocious child. But that doesn't give you permission to speak your mind in class or in public. Watch what you say around others."

I stared at the worn wood floor in need of new varnish before it rotted through. I looked up. "What's the value of education unless I can express my thoughts? You taught me that."

"Regina, I taught you to think for yourself. It's your responsibility to know when not to speak your mind."

"What's the point of learning if I can't speak out against injustice?"

Mo-Mere's eyes bored into me. "You know the answer."

I picked up a Chinese cipher puzzle she set out when we were alone, a tribute to my mother's heritage.

"Well?" Mo-Mere prompted.

"We can't be sure those cast out of the Federation, like Beth, aren't spies."

"It's not just her. There's no telling who might turn you in for speaking out against the Federation."

"How can speaking the truth be wrong?" I asked.

"There's truth and there's integrity." She poured the tea. "For example, if you met the ugliest girl in the world, would you tell her?"

"Only if I wanted a fight."

Mo-Mere laughed. "There you have it." She put two cups of tea on the table with some hard biscuits.

I sat on a wood-stump stool, cradled the hot tea, and stared at a biscuit. Eating her food brought guilt. She had so little. Yet I was hungry and she was willing. I ate because I assumed Mom bartered for this. I sipped the tea, relishing its bittersweet flavor.

Mo-mere pushed aside her stove, raised a trap door, and pulled up a plastic-wrapped package. I wondered what she would surprise me with today.

"You have an active mind." Mo-Mere toweled off and

unwrapped the package. "Promise you'll make good use of your life. Don't let your brain go to waste."

I wanted to remove my brain and hand it to her, since she prized it so much. She could wrap it in plastic like her precious books.

Mo-Mere placed a book with a leather cover on the table. "Why don't we try this: *A Tale of Two Cities*? It's about a time of hardships and spies. You can't let anyone know. The Federation banned this at the highest levels."

I opened the delicate cover to yellowed pages, crisp and brittle to my touch. I held these fragile pages in reverence for the knowledge few except me could read. I spoke aloud to hear the opening words in my ears. "It was the best of times."

While Mo-Mere wrapped the other books, I read to myself. After she'd placed the package beneath the stove, she stood over me. "Read up. I have to go for storm supplies. I'll be back in an hour."

I was torn between reading and joining her to visit barter houses and see what might be available for exchange.

She must have read my mind. "It's too dangerous. A storm brings unsavory characters interested in taking advantage. Besides, you need to expand your mind in order to survive in the Federation."

"They won't want me to know this book."

Mo-Mere smiled. "The purpose of reading isn't to memorize, though you do that very well. It's to widen your perspective, sharpen critical thinking, and to expand your heart. Don't just memorize, though if you commit this to memory and copy it later, the world will be grateful."

"I know."

"And don't get so wrapped up that you lose track of time or surroundings. Keep your ears sharp in case we get company. If for any reason I'm not back in two hours, put the book in the cabinet over the sink basin and take your sister straight home. I don't want you out after dark."

* * *

I absorbed the words a page at a time. Holding the brittle paper, I paused to let the story sift into memory like spud sugar dissolving in tea. I eased over a new leaf in anticipation of more.

In the story, a wide channel like our Barrier Wall separated prosperous England from desperate France. Reading the story made me feel free, unshackled by the Federation, the Department of Antiquities, or the problems of the world beyond the Wall.

I scanned the last page of the book into memory and sat back. Mo-Mere rushed into the apartment. "It's late. You should have left already." She took the book and placed it in her cupboard.

"I sure hope I can do something noble."

"That wasn't the point of the book." Mo-Mere pushed me toward her door. "Not the only point, at least. Don't you dare sacrifice yourself. We'll talk later. Get your boots on and hurry home. Don't forget Colleen."

Pulling on my boots, I recalled the text of Dickens' book to convert it to long-term memory. "Did I do something wrong, Mo-Mere?"

"No." She sighed. "I'd let you stay, but your mother would worry. I have no way to let her know."

"She wouldn't mind. She's always busy."

"Regina, you know better. Besides, patrols are out like black flies. I don't know what they're looking for, but I don't like it. Don't stop for any salvage side trips. Promise you'll go straight home."

I hadn't seen Mo-Mere this angry and scared before.

Colleen was napping in her wood-frame classroom. When I woke her, she looked stunned. "Are we home? Did you forget me again?" She looked around and shook her head. "You got another detention. Why do I have to be punished?"

I tugged on her worn boots. "I'm sorry. We need to hurry."

With the sun fading behind trees on the west side of the island, we headed down the steps. I led the way beside the log stilts that held up the schoolhouse. We reached my hollowed-out log-boat beneath the window to Mo-Mere's classroom.

"Why can't you be like the other girls?" Colleen asked when we reached the shore.

I shrugged and untied the mooring rope. *We can't change our nature.*

Two gray-coated Antiquities agents entered the clearing in front of the school. They were the bogeybeasts we had nightmares about. Yet this was the first time I'd seen them at the school. *Mo-Mere's black flies.*

I helped Colleen into the boat and tossed the rope inside. I shooed a couple of rats that tried to hitch a ride and gave Colleen our Antiquities signal. She huddled low, clutching her turquoise necklace, a gift from Mom. I pushed the boat and slid into the back. Colleen pointed to an alligator surfacing among the cattails and tucked in her arms, making herself small.

When the gray-coats weren't looking, I paddled out onto the muddy channel. Water extended in all directions, dotted with drenched trees, cattails, rush, and other swamp grasses. Small islands rose above the murky waters.

Seeing Antiquities agents at school made me cautious. I steered close to shore, watching for alligators, snakes, and the spare coyote that somehow survived out here. They all made a decent feast, if they didn't eat you first. I'd read that before the Great Collapse, gators had been a shy species, less than a dozen feet long, avoiding humans unless disturbed. To punish us, the Federation introduced crocodile DNA to create larger, more aggressive gators.

I paddled across a channel and hugged the shore of the next island.

"Got you, you little swamp rat," said a terse voice behind me.

Something pinched my neck. My sister stifled a scream and turned to jump overboard. The broad snout of an alligator poked above the water. Colleen dropped back into the log-boat and curled into a ball.

I couldn't move my arms or legs. The paddle fell from my grip and landed at my feet. I couldn't feel anything below my neck. I stared at the charcoal sky. I'd heard of bounty hunters using nerve block when they captured girls, but I never expected to feel it myself.

Someone pulled our boat through the cattails along the shore. She had a clump of ebony hair surrounding a coarse, pockmarked face, and wore the Department of Antiquities emblem on gray uniform. In fact, she had the insignia of the chief inspector.

Intense eyes burned into me. "You can't escape our patrols. We see and hear everything." The Antiquities woman grabbed Colleen's left arm, lifted her, and brandished a needle. "This won't hurt."

Colleen cried out.

"Leave her alone," I said. "She hasn't done anything."

"New regulations." The coarse-faced one pinched my sister's arm and jabbed a huge needle into the puckered skin.

Colleen slumped like a dead squirrel, her head cocked to the side. She whimpered.

I tried to muster my strength to help her, but my muscles failed to respond. "Let her go."

Coarse-face dropped Colleen into the boat and turned to me. "A rebel fighter, eh?"

"No, ma'am."

"Then what's the fuss?" She grabbed my left arm, pinched my skin, and stuck me with her needle.

The jab brought no pain, yet I felt violated. "What are you giving us?"

"A tracking implant, so we can find you later. The nerve block will fade. Then you can be on your way." She drew blood, slapped a bandage over the open sores, and dropped me into my boat.

I fell backward and saw two other gray uniforms. One held a tranquilizer rifle; that must have been what first pinched me.

Coarse-face drew blood from Colleen and put a bandage on her oozing arm. Then the chief inspector joined the other women in an Antiquities speedboat.

"I can't understand where all these girls come from," one of the gray-coats said. "You'd think they'd stop breeding."

Coarse-face rolled her eyes and shook her head. "Maybe the gators will do the job."

"I can't move," I yelled. "At least shoo them away."

* * *

I lay beneath angry black clouds, wanting to kick myself for falling into a patrol trap, but my legs wouldn't move. They must have used infrared to track us. My mistake was believing the shore was too shallow for patrol boats. These agents had a smaller speedboat some patrols attached to their larger boats. I didn't feel blessed for the privilege of the chief inspector's attention.

The gray-coats sped away. I craned my neck to see if any dangerous predators awaited their next meal. "Colleen, you okay?" I barely saw her slumped in front.

"No."

I'd failed her. Mo-Mere had warned me and I couldn't protect Colleen. Rats boarded the boat and scurried down the sides toward her. The gator to my right swam closer.

"Regina!"

"I see them." I grunted, trying to jerk my body awake. My head banged against the log-boat. My arms quivered and fell. My left arm stung where that devil had injected me. *Good. The nerve block must be wearing off.* The bandage from the implant bulged over my wound.

Dark clouds swirled above us, moving west. They threatened to blot out the plum sunset with the beginnings of the storm. Rain fell, a drizzle at first, then heavier. I lay face up with water splashing my eyes, nose, and mouth.

"Regina, they're biting."

"Jump as if something scared you."

She grunted and rocked the log. "It's not helping."

"Don't make another sound." I spotted an alligator nosing the side of the log. All it had to do was bump us just right and we'd spill over, paralyzed.

Clenching my fists, I lifted a leg. It dropped like limp noodles. I did it again. This time, my right arm shot halfway up before it collapsed. One of the rats fell off the log. The gator's long snout shot up. Bone crunched in the gator's jaws.

I kept still, holding my breath. I recalled that the fastest way to cleanse toxins was to get my blood circulating.

Thinking about Antiquities agents did the trick. My heart raced. I tightened my muscles. "Grrr."

"Regina, the rats."

"Raaa!" My arms and legs twitched in the air. I was a turtle on its back. Rats scurried away. The alligator rocked our log. Another rat dropped off, distracting the gator. "Raaa!" My arms and legs moved together. Feeling returned to my toes and fingers.

The alligator snapped, trying to grab my leg. Its lunge scooted our boat into the channel. The gator followed.

"Raaa!" I aimed for a rat and knocked it off. We floated free of the cattails. With my right hand I grabbed a paddle and dropped it. I grabbed again, swung at a rat near Colleen, and knocked it off. Another rat bit the end of the paddle and hung on. I smacked it against the log. The rat let go and scurried toward Colleen.

"Regina!"

Two gators approached from the right, their eyes above the muddy water. I let go of the paddle and pushed myself into a sitting position. My head slumped back like a stone. I shoved a rat from my end of the boat and shooed the ones near Colleen.

The rancid breath of a gator blew in from behind me. Straining to grip the paddle in both hands, I got in a few strokes. That sent us in a wide arc. I switched sides. If it had been only one gator, I might have pulled the crossbow from beneath my seat, but I didn't want to waste arrows. I couldn't afford to lose the bow overboard.

Colleen stirred. "Get these rats off."

"You can move your arms now. When one bites, grab it behind the neck and snap. It'll make for a good dinner tonight."

"Can't you?"

I switched sides and paddled. "Would you rather be a gator's dinner?"

One of the rats bit her leg. She grabbed it and snapped the neck. She threw the body into the middle of the boat and grabbed another by her left shoulder.

"Good girl. Mom will be proud."

"This is your fault, for detention."

Pile on the guilt.

When I'd put enough distance between the gators and us, I helped Colleen with the remaining rats until we had four carcasses. She crawled up into my arms and wept. She hadn't cried until then, brave girl.

I stroked her stringy hair and held her tight, letting her have a good cry while I watched for water snakes.

Colleen dried her eyes and looked up at me. "Don't ever leave me. Promise."

"I promise."

She returned to the front of the boat and helped me paddle toward home. I was tempted to dive for salvage among the sunken homes of Richmond. Most times I came up empty, but once I found specially-coated stainless cookware I bartered for a goat to provide milk.

The rain came harder. Roiling black clouds took over the sky. Colleen feared the dark, and the oncoming storm could trap us. I paddled harder.

* * *

Rain covered us like a soggy blanket. Night terror crept into Colleen's eyes.

Nighttime was the worst. Nocturnal predators came out. Some, like the owls, didn't frighten me, but somehow coyotes made it from island to island like the rats. When they couldn't find birds or smaller mammals, they turned on humans, particularly at night. There were snakes—poisonous cottonmouths, and pythons with powerful muscles that could choke—and they hid well. Hungry gators lurked nearby. One had even wandered into the clearing by our cabin. When she wouldn't leave, we made a good dinner of her, similar to chicken but with tougher meat.

We finally reached the cove of our own tiny island. No smoke came from the chimney, which meant Mom's cooking fire wasn't burning. No lights shined from our cabin. That sent shivers up my spine. We'd have to tie up the log-boat in the dark and feel our way home, hoping to avoid the traps we used to snare food and keep out raiders and scavengers.

In the dark, I pulled my crossbow from beneath my seat and peeled off the plastic sheathing. Then I freed my quiver of short arrows and pulled the boat up behind the reeds.

"Where's Mom?" Colleen asked.

"She's probably out bartering," I whispered. "Be quiet and keep your ears sharp."

In the soggy darkness, I couldn't see Mom's boat. I slung the quiver of arrows over my shoulder and attached the bow. I grabbed the rats by the tails and tucked Colleen's hand to my elbow. Using a stick to test for traps, we moved through tall grass. With no stars in the stormy sky to guide us, we reached the pebbly trail that led up to the leaky log hut we called home.

Colleen clutched my arm; her dread coursed through me. Inching forward, I tested each step with the stick. Something snapped shut with a metallic clank. I froze and listened.

Hearing nothing else through the wind and rain, I lifted the stick, now heavy with its tip in the jaws of a trap. I waved the stick before me and pushed forward, testing the ground twice before moving. When we reached the clearing, lightning illuminated our single-room log cabin. It wasn't hard to find if you kept heading uphill. Colleen squeezed my arm.

A gun clicked.

I reached for my bow to notch an arrow, though a bow was a poor weapon against a gun in the dark, particularly if we faced scavengers with infrared and night vision.

"Mom?" Colleen trembled.

A faint light flickered to my right. "You scared me," Mom said. "I thought you were scavengers." She moved closer. "Where's the cooking fire?" she snapped. "You should have been home hours ago."

"She got detention again," Colleen volunteered and ran to Mom.

"I pay for classes so you can learn, not so you can bother Madam Seville. Find some dry wood and get the fire going." She slung the shotgun over her shoulder.

In the flicker of the light beam, I saw bags under Mom's eyes. I handed her the rats and looked around before she took Colleen and the light inside.

I ran to the side of the cabin, picked up an armful of driftwood I'd cut that morning, and carried it inside. An oil-rag lamp cast faint shadows on the walls. It was too dark to read, but Mom had no books, not even a Mesh-reader with government-approved texts.

"You're lucky patrol agents didn't take you away," Mom said after hearing the tale from Colleen. "From now on, come straight home after school. No more salvage. And make sure those patrols don't follow you. There's work to be done around here."

"Why would patrols take us?" Colleen asked.

"I don't know." Mom glared at me not to say more. "I just don't want to lose you two monkeys." She hugged Colleen.

Mom had me skin the rats. Then she fried them up in a skillet with wild spuds and greens that survived in our garden—a feast, more than we often had on Sundays. Leftovers would make for a good stew.

"Do you have school tomorrow?" she asked.

I nodded.

"Make sure you don't get detention. Is that clear? A terrible storm is brewing. I want you and Colleen home the instant class is over. Don't fail me."

Getting home in an instant would have been impossible without one of the Federation's sky-jumpers, which we could only watch from the ground. I didn't say so. Mom was in enough of a sour mood.

We sat around our tree-stump table. Mom propped her shotgun next to her in case we got visitors. Colleen and I waited until Mom nodded that we could eat. We rarely said prayers. Mom said the Federation prayed to false gods and praying to anyone else risked arrest and days without food in a Marginal prison cage.

I looked into her sunken eyes. "Thanks, Mom, for giving us a good home."

She looked up and smiled, which did little to soften her sadness.

"Thank you for providing dinner."

That sounded like a Marginal barter exchange, which saddened me. I often wondered what her life might have been without us. Was I keeping her from doing better? She took no joy in having children, me at least. Yet this weight of guilt didn't originate with her. It came from reading stories from other times and places.

Unlike Mo-Mere, who used every moment to teach, Mom didn't let us talk over dinner. She hadn't in a very long time. Like Federation Elites, she didn't like me asking questions. When I'd asked about her past and my donor mother, she distracted me with chores. Six months ago, we stopped talking altogether, except when we couldn't avoid it. I didn't know how to bridge the growing rift between us.

After dinner, Mom put leftovers in a stainless container I'd salvaged. While Colleen climbed onto her cot across from the kitchen and pretended to sleep, Mom locked the doors and windows and filled canvas bags for the next day.

I hated storms. They meant leaving home to hunt for higher ground. The worst part was sitting around listening to the winds and rain pounding us, wondering if that storm would take our cabin. We'd been fortunate so far, but Mom's eyes looked weary, as if she knew something about this hurricane.

Her gloom heightened my need for answers; I might not get another chance. I ached to learn about my donor mother and why Colleen and I looked dissimilar, with different Hispanic features as well as Mom's Chinese ones. She'd told me our donor was a Hispanic woman who died of some mutating disease they couldn't cure. I had no memories of her. Mom even refused to tell me her name, as if shame worse than being Marginals had befallen our family.

I approached Mom. Before I could frame a question, she said, "Check the water tanks."

Deflated, I pulled on my boots.

"While you're out, pick some fruit. We'll need it."

In the dark rain, I went to the water system Mom and I had built to bring muddy water up from the channel into a holding tank. Next to that, we made a small boiling chamber over a wood stove to use when we could find dry wood. The evaporated water went through a compressor and a counter-flow heat exchanger that transferred heat from cleaned water to incoming channel water. As a result, we had fresh water for the kitchen basin and for taking quick, cool showers.

To save firewood, I used the foot pump to fill the river tank. Then I put sheltered wood into the cast-iron burner so we would have fresh water in the morning. On my way into the cabin I remembered the fruit. We had an orange tree on the northeast side of the clearing for maximum sunlight, and an apple tree with a little more afternoon shade.

Rain streamed down my cheeks. I wiped my eyes and found the orange tree by light seeping through the cabin's drapes. I listened for scavengers or gators, and strained to see if snakes nested in the tree.

Taking a deep breath, I rolled up my canvas shirt and reached up. My hand brushed through leaves and settled on an orange, firm and ripe. Something slithered onto my arm. I brushed it away and grabbed the orange.

I waved my hand through the leaves until I found a second orange, but it was too small. A third didn't feel ripe. After finding two ripe ones close together, I plucked them and wrapped them in my drenched canvas top. I found another and decided four would be enough for four days.

Nearby was the apple tree. I only found two apples low enough to pick, and they were probably green. I picked them anyhow. A snake dropped onto my shoulders and curled around me. Holding the fruit with my left hand, I headed for the cabin and grabbed hold of snake muscle as thick as my thumb. By cabin light, I saw I had the head, and thankfully it wasn't a python or a cottonmouth. The snake's body coiled around my arm and neck.

I placed the fruit on the porch, pulled a knife from my belt, and sliced through the snake's head. Its body tightened around me. The head hung by a strand of muscle and then came loose. I threw it into the clearing, dropped the knife next to the fruit, and uncoiled the ropelike creature from my neck. After attaching the knife to my belt and gathering up the apples and oranges in my soaked top, I grabbed the snake and entered the cabin. I placed my spoils on the tree stump table.

Mom nodded at the snake and kissed my forehead. "You're a good girl. That'll give us something for tomorrow. Never let your guard down. Not for a moment. I'm not angry. I'm worried … for both of you. Today the patrols got too close. Don't ever let them take you."

"I know, Mom."

Guilt was worse than the rare times she yelled at me.

I pulled off my boots, stacked them by the door, and dried off with terrycloth. Then I changed my canvas clothes and crawled onto my cot in the corner next to Colleen. She was snoring.

I removed the bandage from my left arm. The swelling had gone down. It felt like a wasp sting with an ugly red spot in the middle. I wanted to dig out the tracking chip, but I'd heard that brought the severe penalty of swamp prison, where you had to fight off snakes and rats impatient for you to die.

* * *

In the morning, dark, angry clouds pushed in from the north, bringing cooler air. Colleen and I were soaked by the time we reached school.

"Sorry, dear," Mo-Mere said from the school doorway. "I cancelled classes so students could help their families prepare."

"But it's Friday."

"They're calling this the storm of the century."

Because we lived farthest from school, we were the last to know. "That's what they said last year," I told her. I tugged at my wet, muddy boots.

Mo-Mere lifted my chin. "I'd love to let you dry out and read, but you need to go home and prepare. This could be the big one legends warned about."

"I thought that was Federation propaganda."

"Take Colleen home before the channel becomes impassible."

I hung my head. "Patrols grabbed us on the way home yesterday."

Mo-Mere sighed and rolled up the loose ragged canvas of my sleeve to examine my arm. She disappeared into her apartment and returned with ointment and a fresh bandage. "This should help it heal." Her face turned gloomy, like the sky.

"Why would the Department care what happens to us? I mean, we're outside the Federation."

"Usually they don't, which makes this highly unusual."

"Is that why they came to school yesterday? Is that why you cancelled?"

Mo-Mere nodded. "Hurry home. Stay clear of patrols. Nothing good comes from dealing with them. Get to the highest ground and grab hold of anything that won't float you out to sea. Good luck."

"Where will you go?"

"Don't worry about me. Just take care of Colleen and your mom." She pushed a small package of crackers into my hand and kissed my forehead.

I hugged Mo-Mere as if even then, I knew this storm would change everything. I imprinted her face in my memory.

Outside, Colleen stood in the rain; her dark hair drooped around her face. "Tell me you didn't get detention."

"Not today, you drowned rat."

She ran up the rickety wooden steps and pretended to hit me. Instead, she took my hand. I waved to Mo-Mere and lingered until she went inside. I looked at six other classroom/apartments on stilts clustered around a growing muddy pond. Then I led Colleen to our log-boat.

Waters rose as I paddled out into the channel. The rush and cattails didn't hide as much of the horizon as they had the day before. The shoreline on either side grew farther away. The current was stronger, making it hard to move upstream.

"Come on, Colleen. If you help, we'll get home sooner."

She grumbled but took the front paddle.

At least the alligators made themselves scarce. Snakes slithered by on frothy waters. One washed into the boat. Its markings were those Mo-Mere had shown us as a baby python. When it got bigger, it could choke the life out of you. I looked for its mother.

Water rose within our boat but the log would float. I kept moving. The snake slithered out. Broken branches floated by along with mud-caked log bundles, some tarred to keep out weather. Another bundle headed toward us.

"Starboard," I yelled.

We paddled hard off the port side, sending us in an arc. The bundle of logs smacked the back of our boat, pushing us close to rocks.

"Port," I yelled. We paddled the other side.

The boat bounced against rocks and spun around, facing out to sea.

"Turn and head the other way," I said. The nice thing about my log-boat was that either end could be the bow.

The center of the channel grew frothy, the current strong. We had to stay close to shore, risking rocks, debris, and whatever else lurked in the shallows.

Through the curtain of thick rain, I spotted a patrol boat skulking in the seaward channels. It kept its distance from floating debris. Already this storm felt like the King James Bible, threatening a flood that was growing faster than any I'd seen before. It was as if a dam had burst.

I pulled close to an island and crossed the channel, using the land and trees as a shield from the patrol. Out in the middle, the channel pushed us downstream. We had to paddle hard to get to the other side and retrace our way upstream. My arms ached, but we couldn't let up.

Behind me, red-faced Colleen splashed at the water, barely countering my strokes to keep us straight. I found a cove away from the main current where I turned the boat around so I could watch her and what lay ahead.

"Can we rest?" she asked.

"Wouldn't you rather get home?"

She nodded and put her paddle into the water. "Home."

I didn't mention the patrol.

* * *

It seemed to take forever, but we avoided the patrol and made it home. Mom stood in the cove preparing her rectangular flat-bottomed skiff. Her hair draped around her round cheeks like a wet rag.

"I was coming to get you," she said. "Grab your things. We have to move upstream. Waters are rising too fast, and this is just the beginning."

Rain fell hard as hail, pounding my head and back. Mom had loaded the skiff with the stainless container of leftovers, along with bundles I took to be food and our bedding wrapped in reclaimed plastic. I helped her secure the last packages to the frame.

Packets filled every space. Mom must have figured we'd never return. *No time to dwell.*

With all the supplies, the skiff rode low in the water. Waves washed over the side. I looked up the hill for a glimpse of the cabin, trying to think of what else I could rescue.

"Let's go," Mom said.

I climbed in next to Colleen and handed her a bucket. "We need to bail or we'll sink." I tied the cord from the bucket around her wrist so it wouldn't fly away.

Mom pushed the skiff away from the cove, and sat facing me.

"Where to?" I asked, tying my bucket to my seat.

When we were out in the channel, she rowed upstream. Muscles in her arms rippled with each stroke. "A friend, Vera Morton agreed to take us in. They have another ten feet on us."

I sensed her saying a prayer, as all families did during storms that the waters didn't take more than we could afford to lose, which wasn't much. While she rowed, I pointed away from rocks and debris, and helped Colleen bail. We barely kept up with the sheets of rain filling the boat.

When the current pushed Mom too close to shore, I wiped rain from my face and pointed upstream. A wave washed over the side of the skiff. I kept scooping out water. Mom's face grew weary. Her strokes slowed until I feared we weren't keeping up with the angry current.

"I can row," I said.

"Keep bailing."

The sky grew dark as twilight. With winds coming from the northeast and no rudder, it was hard for Mom to keep us on the right path. Easterly gusts churned the waters. This was the dangerous time, when a wall of water could capsize us, sending our boat crashing against trees and rocks. I'd seen that in the last big storm, causing a wreck with no survivors.

Lightning flashed. Rain pelted us from the northeast. I took a spare oar and leaned over the side.

"Navigate," Mom said. "And bail."

"The current's too strong," I yelled over the howling wind. "We won't make it."

"Don't talk like that." Her voice strained. I could almost feel Mom reaching out to grab me and Colleen. "I won't have my daughters defeated," she said. "Do you hear? No matter what happens to me, survive this. I have *not* sacrificed for you two to give up."

Colleen bailed faster. "I'm not giving up, Mom. I promise. I won't."

Yet she was growing tired. We all were.

The winds picked up out of the east. Rain pounded harder,

coming horizontally. Yet we were fighting current from the west. That gave me an idea.

I tied the skiff's stern mooring rope around my waist, pulled a sheet from one of Mom's bundles, and tied two ends to my feet. Holding up the other two corners, I stood and let my body and the sheet act as a sail. Rain slapped my face. My mouth and nose filled with water. I gagged and coughed. We caught the wind, moved away from a nearby shore, then up the channel.

My legs strained to keep standing. Cramps gripped my calf muscles. My arms fought to hold the sheet out for maximum sail. Shaking, I held that position until I couldn't get a breath. I dropped into my seat, checked my compass, and helped Colleen bail.

Legs burned, arms ached. I stood again and fought the wind. I coughed, took a deep breath with too much water, and coughed again. At least the rain cleansed the air. My giggly classmates would say that was unnatural. Yet these cleansings sharpened my senses to the crowded aromas of the swamps, odors that could warn of danger. That reverie gave me strength to push through pain and fatigue.

I took a break to help Colleen bail and stood again, struggling to maintain my balance against the pull of nature. Lightning struck nearby. A tree sparked. The pungent odor of ozone filled my sinuses. Rain doused the fire before the tree could light up the sky. Shorn branches tumbled into the rising waters.

Wind howled in my ears, a deafening cry announcing that this was the end. This flood would cleanse the world of Marginal swamp rats and wash us out to sea for our sins against the Community Movement. That was what the Federation taught us. We were the cursed ones, the damned. *Well, damn them.*

Mom didn't scold me. She didn't yell at me to stop and bail. I smiled and pushed through the pain.

* * *

I was still standing, shaking, and struggling to breathe when the skiff came to an abrupt stop. The rope saved me from falling toward the bow. I dropped the soaked sheet, collapsed onto my seat, and looked around. Clouds had turned charcoal black, closing in around us. We were in a cove, away from the river's rising current, a new inlet that hadn't existed before this storm.

Mom tied the front of the skiff to a tree trunk and returned to help me up. "You did great, dear. I'm so proud of you." She held me in her arms with rain cascading over us. "You saved us. You did."

When she let go, I slumped into my seat. Rain splattered Colleen's ashen face, matting her chocolate hair against her cheeks. Mom lifted her out of the skiff and led her up the rocky hill. I climbed out, untied two plastic-covered bundles from the skiff's rail, and struggled to carry them uphill. Rain-slick rocks slowed my climb. Rivulets of water raced toward the shore. I tripped, dropped my load, and braced to protect my head.

Covered in mud, I reached the top of the hill. A log cabin stood at the highest point, next to two other homes across a small clearing. I trudged forward under the weight of the bundles. My rubbery legs threatened to collapse. A big woman burst out of the nearest cabin. A porch light shining on her face showed frizzy brown hair and mysterious dark eyes. She aimed a flashlight toward me.

"You must be Regina. Bless you. You're a very brave girl. Go inside and get dry. Oh, and call me Aunt Vera."

With her cape over her head, she hurried down to the skiff. I went in and dropped my bundles by the door. A young version of Vera greeted me. "Give me your boots and clothes, and we'll dry them by the fireplace."

They had an actual stone fireplace, where Mom and Colleen sat in their underwear. I added my clothes to the pile and joined them. The girl who'd greeted me approached with a younger girl who looked to be her sister. They both had dark, tanned skin, tar-black hair, and elongated faces.

"I'm Jasmine," the older girl said, "and this is Aimee." She acted as if she knew me, though I didn't recall seeing either of them before.

"What was it like out there?" Aimee asked with too much enthusiasm.

"You don't want to go out."

"Your mom said you acted like a human sail. That sounds exciting."

"The wind was too strong. If our skiff hadn't been so heavy, we might have flipped." I didn't want her getting any ideas.

"Come on, you little worm," Jasmine told her sister. "Let's get dinner ready."

I dropped next to Mom, who held Colleen. They both looked

okay, though exhausted. *Try fighting the wind.*

Aunt Vera made several trips while I stayed rooted to the spot, wondering how our home would fare. We'd sustained water damage and erosion last year. Mo-Mere said it was only a matter of time. Marginal life was all about eating away of the land, corrosion of our bodies, wasting away of the population, and a wearing down of our spirits, if we let it.

After locking the door, Aunt Vera hung up her wet clothes and set out six plates on a long table that wouldn't have fit in our home.

Mom and Colleen stood behind empty seats, Mom the farthest from the kitchen. I joined them and stood across from Jasmine. "Thanks for helping us," I said to be polite. I wondered how much Mom had bartered for this.

Vera smiled and sat closest to the kitchen. "We need to stick together and help each other during tough times. This has to be the worst storm I've seen." She passed out plates heaped with catfish and spuds.

Mom nodded. "That wind is coming right up the channel."

"We should expect storm surges," Vera said. "Last time it almost washed our boats out to sea. Then what would we do? Eat hearty. We mustn't waste good food."

"We should take extra precautions," Mom said. "Could you watch my girls? I need to check upstream."

"Your family's always welcome. It'll be nice to have company."

It sounded as if they'd planned this and chose that moment to announce it to Colleen and me. "Mom, please don't go without us." Something told me this was different than other times she'd left me with Colleen.

"You should be safe until I return. Now eat. And mind Aunt Vera as you would me."

Not having eaten since dinner last night, I dug into the catfish first, for the protein. I had the notion of having seen Vera long ago, maybe while bartering. I couldn't be sure.

"Make sure to pack everything tonight," Vera said. "It pays to be prepared."

"My stuff's already packed," Jasmine said with pride.

"So is mine," Aimee said.

I rolled my eyes. What kiss-ups.

"Mom, family should stick together at times like this." I talked around a mouthful of fish, better seasoned than anything we had at home. "You know how tough the rowing was."

"I need to make inquiries. Without bundles and passengers, rowing will be easier."

"The Federation forbids us going near the Wall."

Mom patted my hand. "Don't worry, dear. Eat up. You need your strength."

"When are you leaving?" I asked.

"In the morning. Stop fussing. Not another word."

As at home, we ate in silence. I got the impression Vera's family talked over meals, because she gave her daughters a stern look. They stared at their plates while they ate. It had to be Mom, afraid we might say something that would condemn us. Already, I felt the void of her leaving.

After dinner, Mom gave me a long hug. It was like saying good-bye to Mo-Mere. Mom's eyes looked too dark, the shadows beneath them growing as if they might swallow her vision.

"Get some sleep," she said. "We'll talk later."

* * *

Colleen and I lay on cots in the corner of the big room opposite the kitchen. Aunt Vera sent her daughters into their bedroom and extinguished the oil-rag lamp, plunging us into darkness. "Don't want the winds blowing it over and setting the house on fire," she said.

She took Mom into the other bedroom. I heard them whispering, but couldn't make out what they said, only that they both sounded worried. Colleen, who didn't like the dark even on a calm night, moved her cot next to mine. Still it took her a long time to fall asleep.

The storm battered the house all night, letting up for a moment, then howling louder than before. Damp air wormed its way through cracks in the tarred log walls and around windows, pushing its clamminess along the east side of the great hall.

The storm still raging when I woke early, feeling as if I hadn't slept. I got ready to do chores before school.

It took a moment to realize weren't at home. There would be no school on account of the storm. My thin sheet was soaked, as was Colleen's and the floor around us. Across the room, Mom's bedding was gone.

I slid off my cot onto the wet wood floor and crossed the room looking for where she might have gone to stay dry. "Mom," I whispered. Her backpack was gone.

Winds rattled windows and the cabin's frame. Spray hit my face through cracks in the wall. I stuffed bits of rag, but it was hopeless. Puddles pooled across the floor. I knocked on Aunt Vera's door.

"What is it, child?" She opened the door, wearing the same green canvas from the night before.

"Mom's gone."

Vera nodded. "She didn't want to disturb you. She went upriver to scout higher ground. I promised to look after you."

"She left us." My stomach twitched. She'd never gone during a storm before. I tensed my muscles to keep from sobbing.

Aunt Vera held me. "It'll be okay. I'm sure she'll be back soon."

I pushed away, ran to the front door, and opened it to a scene of horror. Waves broke against the base of the porch as if the house had become its own island. When they retreated, they dragged part of the vegetable garden with them. Rain pelted my face.

"Water's up to the steps," I said.

Aunt Vera joined me in the doorway and gasped. "Gather your things. We have to go."

"We can't," I said. "We have to wait for Mom."

"No time." Vera hurried into her daughters' room.

Colleen stirred. "Where's Mom?"

"I don't know," Aunt Vera said, returning with bags. *A lie.* Mom must have said something last night.

Aunt Vera gathered bags by the front door while I helped Colleen with hers.

Jasmine came in, rubbing her eyes. "Why do I only get two bags?"

"Only what you can carry," Vera said. "Quick."

Aimee carried her bag to the door, dropped it in a puddle, and joined Colleen. "That's a pretty necklace. Are the stones real?" Mom had given Colleen the long turquoise string of beads for her last birthday. Colleen hadn't taken it off, even to shower.

I pulled Mom's bundles toward the door. "Why are the waters rising so fast?"

"Federation must be pumping water our way. No more questions."

Loud pounding at the door sounded above the din of the wind and rain. A leather-faced woman, with her hair tied under a waterproof hat, barged in. She must have been from one of the other cabins.

"Boat's ready," she said. "We leave in five. Can I help carry?"

Vera pointed to bags her girls had placed by the door. "Regina, this is Aunt Yvonne. She has a motorboat we'll take upriver to meet your mom. Let's go. Quick, quick."

Jasmine and Aimee each wore a backpack. I pulled on mine, helped Colleen with hers, and grabbed two of Mom's plastic-wrapped bundles. Aimee grinned with excitement, not a lick of fear in her. Jasmine looked scared for both of them. I couldn't believe we had to flee our refuge.

Colleen squeezed the turquoise necklace dangling lose around her neck. "Is Mom coming back?" Her face hardened as she tried to act brave.

"We'll meet her along the way." I forced a smile and led her toward the open door. Waves lapped the stairs leading up to the wooden porch. Waters were rising much faster than last time. All our things back home would be soaked, ruined. Our poor goat remained tethered to a tree behind our house. We should have brought her, but there wasn't room in the skiff. Now we would have no milk and nothing to barter except our backpacks and Mom's wrapped bundles.

The moment we stepped outside, the winds blew me against the side of the cabin and knocked Colleen backward. The necklace flopped over her shoulder and caught on her chin. She grabbed it and dropped her bundle. I grabbed her package and the railing. Then I pulled myself and Colleen down the steps into calf-deep water. The boat bobbed behind the middle cabin with water behind it as far as I could see, as if this were the last stretch of land before the open seas. And I was looking upstream.

How could Mom leave? Family is everything. I hoped she was okay and whatever caused her to go was worth it.

I fought tightness in my gut and moved forward. Rain washed away any tears. Mom had dropped us like so much useless salvage, and we threw almost nothing away. Were we less useful than her precious salvage goods? Maybe it wasn't fair to accuse Mom, but I felt betrayed at how distant she'd become. For months she'd withdrawn, as if Colleen and I were too much burden. She worried constantly about not finding enough salvage to barter. Now she was gone.

Colleen stumbled. Yvonne carried her onto the boat. I sloshed through water that filled my thin boots. I lost my footing, gulped air, and went under. I clutched my bundles, refusing to let go of our few remaining possessions. I wasn't sure what was in the packages, just that they were ours and it was my job to protect them.

Aunt Yvonne grabbed hold of me and helped me up. She handed the plastic-wrapped packages to Aunt Vera and helped me onto the boat.

The vessel was big. Colleen and I stood on the upper deck looking at the swirling seas. Aunt Vera took her girls to the covered lower deck. Another woman I took to be the mother of a third family nudged three girls Colleen's age and younger below.

From the deck I bore witness to the end of the only world I knew. We weren't on Noah's ark, but it would have to do. Waves battered the boat against a rocky ledge that threatened to destroy us. Choppy water splashed over the sides. Winds pushed upriver, while the rain kept coming.

Aunt Yvonne untied ropes that moored the boat to a tree and looked up at the same instant I saw it: a big gray boat heading our way. The cruiser had the distinct markings of the Department of Antiquities, along with one of their quiet inboard motors. In the last storm they and their bounty hunter friends kidnapped dozens of girls to sell across the Barrier Wall as farm, mine, and factory slaves. When questioned afterward, agents claimed those girls had died in the storm. Yet I'd watched them being carted off.

Behind the patrol boat, a wall of water pushed its way up the channel.

Yvonne crawled aboard next to me and called to the woman at the helm: "Patrols! Surge! Head west."

I pulled Colleen toward the steps leading down. The boat rocked, sending her sprawling across the deck. I reached for her hand.

The wall of water hit the cluster of homes, splintering them like twigs. That could have been us. The cabins dulled the wave's appetite as the boat sped away. Then the water crashed around the back of the island and hit us from both sides. I held tight to the railing and reached for my sister. She slid down the deck toward the bow and then washed toward the stern, yelling all the way. I grabbed hold of her arm and pulled her to the railing. She let go of the necklace and clung to me. The necklace bounced over her head, arcing across the water.

"No!" she cried. "Mommy's necklace. I can't lose her."

I pressed Colleen's hands to the railing and reached for her precious keepsake. Waves flung the boat sideways. I lost my footing and tumbled over the railing, feet over head. I gulped air before hitting the water and tumbled. I couldn't find up. My lungs burned. The waters tossed me like bubbles in a boiling pot. I finally surfaced, gasping for air. The boat pulled away.

At the railing, Yvonne held Colleen, who cried out, "Regina, don't leave me." Colleen reached out as if she could pluck me from the water. The current pulled me under. I swam back to the surface.

The wind picked up and swallowed all further traces of their voices. I swam to no avail. Then I treaded water, waiting for the boat to return. It didn't slow, didn't turn around. A wave crested. The patrol boat still headed our way.

I'm here. Come back.

With the patrol in pursuit, Vera's boat wasn't coming back. First Mom left, now Vera. I clenched my fists and realized I held something: Colleen's turquoise necklace. Somewhere in all that tumbling, I'd grabbed it and held on. I tucked it into my pocket and watched Vera's boat disappear beyond my reach.

I was on my own.

* * *

After the surge, the waters retreated, sucking everything out to sea. Soon they would threaten again. They always did while the winds raged up the channel. Staying put was a recipe for death. I wasn't ready to die. I couldn't. My job was to protect Colleen.

"Stop feeling sorry for yourself," Mo-Mere would say. *Focus.*

I turned toward the much smaller island where Aunt Vera and the others lived. The house in the middle was gone, down to a few support beams. The one on the right lacked a roof. Aunt Vera's home stood, though it leaned to the side.

The current pulled me alongside the island, toward the sea. I wasn't strong enough to swim in the ocean, and besides, farther out were sharks and vicious crocodiles.

I dove under the waves and swam hard westward, counting on

the current to bring me closer to the island. I came up for air and tried again. I reached an eddy where the water couldn't decide which side of the island to take, and swam to shore, to what had been the back porch of the middle house. I dragged myself up onto the floorboards.

Another wave crashed over me. *Enough.*

Holding my breath, I clung to battered floorboards. Water tugged me upstream. I didn't let go. When the water retreated, it settled higher than before but left me above the surface. I gulped air. All this water brought a tremendous thirst, yet I'd watched girls drink unfiltered channel water and get ill. I didn't drink.

The retreating wave took part of the third cabin with it. I sloshed through calf-deep water to Aunt Vera's home to look for anything salvageable that would help me survive. The front door was gone, the porch shattered. The cabin itself looked ready to collapse. I had to find something to eat and drink, and secure a boat. I looked for the kitchen.

Water crashed through the doorway, shattered a window, and sent me sliding toward the back of the cabin. I braced against the bedroom doorway while a torrent of winds and water shoved the cabin in several directions.

When that subsided, I waded to the kitchen cupboard. A few jugs of drinking water remained. I gulped one, fastened the top, and tucked the empty under my canvas shirt. I took a second jug, drank some, and attached it to my belt. Beside the sink basin, I found soggy biscuits. It wasn't Mo-Mere's turtle soup, but it would have to do as breakfast. I hoped my teacher had reached safety. She would know what to do.

Vera had taken most of the food. In the bedrooms, clothes sloshed in inches of water around soaked beds. I didn't have a boat or any way to carry them to safety.

The next wave hit and tugged my feet from under me. Walls swayed. I struggled to stay afloat, and then swam, holding on to whatever I could. When the waters pulled away, I clung to the front doorframe. I needed a boat, some way to move to other islands. Yvonne's craft was gone, so was Mom's skiff. All that remained were floating debris—lots of logs—and a coil of rope. Rope was a vital survival tool, so I wrapped some around my waist and knotted it.

Another wave headed toward the cabin. I pushed away from the front door, reached Vera's bedroom, and clung to the doorframe. The wave broke over the porch. The front wall disintegrated, leaving only the front doorframe.

The entire cabin tilted backward with a screeching groan. Waters retreated, pulling the bedroom doorframe and wall forward like brittle pages in a book. Wood splintered and creaked in pain. The bedroom wall gave way and slid toward the front of the cabin, dragging me with it. I grabbed hold of the front doorframe and held on, trying to keep my head above water.

With no support, the roof scraped down what was left of the side walls, hit the doorframe, and splintered wood around me. I slid underwater, under the roof.

No matter how many storms I'd survived, nothing prepared me for the next. Each was different, with its own character. Some were quick, reminding us what it meant to be Marginal. Others lingered as if enjoying the misery they brought. Some were hungry, gobbling up land and possessions. Others were vicious, demanding human and animal sacrifices. Each extracted something special as a toll for survival.

Water tugged me and the cabin. I couldn't get out from under the roof. I found an air pocket and sucked in all I could. Retreating waves shifted the roof and pulled me beneath it, toward the open sea.

After the roof cleared the porch, I pushed myself to the edge, grabbed hold, and pulled my chin above water. I was holding on to a piece of cabin wall, a bundle of logs bound by rope and tar. The shattered remains of Vera's cabin floated alongside me. Little was left of the island except a few trees and bushes that stubbornly held on. They bowed in deference to the waves. All the bartering for materials, and months of labor to build, had vanished in one flood. There was nothing I could do. Vera's island was higher than ours. My home had no chance.

Waves bobbed me up and down. The waters retreated, revealing the bare foundations of three cabins. Behind them, the patrol broke off its pursuit of Aunt Yvonne's boat and navigated around clusters of branches and wreckage. It made no sense for a patrol boat to be so close to debris, taking risks during the worst of the storm. They usually left that for their bounty hunters.

Bits of cabin surrounded me, along with clothing and branches. My bundle of logs was twice my height in length, half that in width—and it floated. I had that, at least. The river moved too fast with too much debris to swim back to Vera's island. Besides, there wasn't a boat. Instead, I floated out to sea with little water or food, no fishing line, and little hope of finding any.

Another wave rolled up the channel, dragging the raft in the undertow before it. I clung tight to the upstream side of the logs and took a deep breath. The wave washed over me, jostling the raft. When I surfaced and looked forward, I didn't see any of the islands that once dotted the channels, just telltale treetops swaying in waves, hinting of lost homes.

Behind me, the patrol boat headed my way. *Toward me!*

What was going on? Was this the same Coarse-face who grabbed Colleen and jabbed needles into our arms? I couldn't outrun a patrol.

The rain pounded so hard I could barely see. My nose and mouth filled with spray coming at me sideways from the east. I felt as if I were drowning in spite of my raft.

Whenever waves crested, the patrol boat appeared closer. It had to be tracking me. Otherwise, why brave the debris and waves battering their boat? *Why me? Are you coming to rescue me? Did you see me fall overboard?*

No, they couldn't have seen me in the cabin. It had to be the chip Coarse-face jabbed into my arm. I hated that woman. Yet she could save me from dehydration, hunger, drowning, and sharks. She was my last hope. I waved my arms.

Mo-Mere's voice resonated in my head. "Avoid Antiquities patrols no matter what." Coarse-face hadn't been interested in our welfare when she'd left us paralyzed, surrounded by gators and rats. Mom said we were lucky patrols hadn't taken us. My head cleared. Patrols kidnapped girls to sell beyond the Wall. They wanted to make money off me. I wouldn't let that woman get her hands on me again.

I climbed into the water, draped my left arm over the corner of the raft, and clutched the end log. Keeping my head above the surface was hard. I loosened the loop of bandage from my upper arm and pushed it down my arm. I risked infection, but I couldn't let them catch me and send me away.

The swelling had gone down, but the puncture hole remained visible. From my belt, I tugged my utility knife. I dug part of the blade into the raft to help open it, and cringed—another wave was coming. Holding my breath, I clung to the log and my knife.

After the raft surfaced, I gasped for air and looked around. The patrol boat raced into the wave. Hand trembling, I pressed the point of the blade against my flesh. I clung to the raft. When the water crested, the patrol boat had braved the wave and turned toward me. I bit back tears. *Mom, why did you leave?*

Clenching my teeth, I stabbed the blade into my upper arm. *Ahgh. Damn, damn, it hurts.* My breathing turned shallow. The stab was much worse than when Coarse-face injected the chip. She'd paralyzed me first with her tranquilizer gun. I pushed the knife point beneath the implanted chip and dug it out, letting it rest on my arm. Smaller than an apple seed, the chip seemed too tiny to cause all this trouble.

My arm throbbed. I closed the knife and fastened it to my belt. Water splashed the open wound. I grabbed the implant chip before it sank, rinsed off my blood, and clenched it between my teeth. I peeled a splinter from a raft log, dug a groove with my thumb, and forced the chip in. Then I set it afloat, pushing it away. *You won't catch me that easily.*

Grrr. My arm stung like a toothache. Blood oozed from my wound. I hadn't thought this through. The scent of blood would attract gators, sharks, and other critters.

I wanted to undo what I'd done. *Too late.*

To stop the bleeding, I pulled the bandage over the wound. Leaning back, I took a deep breath to steady my nerves. The wood chip with my tracking chip floated nearby, too close.

The patrol boat closed in. I pushed water toward the chip, but everything was floating toward the sea. Another wave washed over me. I scrambled to the surface, gasped for air, and hugged the raft. I no longer saw the splinter with my chip. The patrol boat slowed and inched closer. I needed somewhere to hide.

All I saw above water were treetops. This storm had flooded our home as prior storms had taken families farther east. I hoped the gators took refuge in calmer waters. I looked around and didn't see any, but then, they hung low in the water.

I was tempted to let the patrol boat catch me. They might feed me and fix my wounds. But I'd removed my tracking chip. That brought punishments worse than becoming a farm or factory slave. *You did it this time, Regina.*

The patrol boat motored closer. I slipped lower in the water between chunks of cabin wall and tucked my legs up. I pretended to be a gator with only my nose and eyes above water. When the patrol boat pulled next to my raft, I took a deep breath and ducked under water.

The image of the boat etched in my mind. Two gray-uniformed agents scanned with binoculars. Eleven girls in soaked green canvas stood chained to the railing. Two were giggly girls from my class.

A third Antiquities agent stood along the starboard side: the coarse-faced devil. I wondered if she could tell from my tracking device whether I was dead or alive, and whether the device was still in my arm. I stayed near the edge of the raft, listening.

"I don't see any live ones," one of the agents said.

"Keep looking." Coarse-face's voice carried a hint of Marginal twang. "This girl is of vital interest."

I couldn't imagine why. Had they overheard me speaking out at school?

The patrol boat puttered around my floating logs. I waited until my lungs were ready to burst before I surfaced. Who was I kidding? I couldn't survive on the ocean by myself. "Wait." My thin voice vanished on the wind. Panicked, I started to climb onto my raft so I could scream for them to return.

Wait, I said to myself.

My mind replayed images of the Marginal girls chained to the railing. They didn't look happy or saved. The giggly ones looked terrified. I thought of Robert Louis Stevenson's *Kidnapped* and refused to join them.

■ ■ ■

OTHER STORIES BY LANCE ERLICK

REGINA SHEN: RESILIENCE (Regina Shen book 1)

Outcast Regina Shen is forced by the World Federation to live on the seaward side of barrier walls built to hold back rising seas from abrupt climate change. A hurricane threatens to destroy what's left of her world, tearing Regina from her family.

Global fertility has collapsed. Chief Inspector Joanne Demarco of the notorious Department of Antiquities believes Regina holds the key to avoid extinction. Regina fights to stay alive and avoid capture while hunting for her family. Does she have the resilience to survive?

REGINA SHEN: VIGILANCE (Regina Shen book 2)

Regina Shen is pursued by the notorious Department of Antiquities for her unique DNA. She jumps the Barrier Wall into the Federation to find her kidnapped sister. Stuck on a heavily guarded closed university campus in the mountains, she must use her wits to escape and rescue her sister without letting either of two rival Antiquities inspectors capture her.

REGINA SHEN: DEFIANCE (Regina Shen book 3)

Outcast Regina Shen has DNA the Federation believes can reverse a global fertility collapse. Rival Federation agents fight over capturing Regina to gain power amidst turmoil over who will become the new World Premier. Regina has to flee from Virginia through desert and wilderness to Alaska to hunt a treasure big enough to barter for her freedom and that of her sister.

THE REBEL WITHIN (Rebel Series book 1)

Annabelle Scott lives under the iron rule of a female-dominated régime that forces males to fight to the death to train the military elite. When pressed into service as a mechanized warrior to capture escaped boys, Annabelle stays true to herself by helping some escape. Her defiance endangers everyone she loves and thrusts her to a place of impossible life and death decisions.

THE REBEL TRAP (Rebel Series book 2)

Despite being a military recruit, Annabelle Scott rebels against her female-dominated régime by refusing to kill a handsome boy she fancies and helping him escape. Auditory implants and cameras allow her commander to watch her 24-7. Can she help the boy free his brother from a heavily guarded geek institute without destroying her family or getting killed?

Written as a standalone story, *The Rebel Trap* follows Annabelle's adventures from *The Rebel Within*.

REBELS DIVIDED (Rebel Series book 3)

The first time Geo sees Annabelle, they meet as enemies and she doesn't kill him, which mystifies them both. It's after the 2nd Civil War with the nation divided into an all-female Federal Union and a warlord controlled Outland. The Outland warlord kidnaps Annabelle's sister and kills Geo's pa. Can Annabelle and Geo overcome mutual distrust and work together to rescue her sister and gain justice for his pa's murder? And will their feelings for each other derail or further their goals?

Written as a standalone story, *Rebels Divided* is also part of the Rebel series, three years later.

ABOUT THE AUTHOR

Lance Erlick writes science fiction thrillers for young adult and adult readers. He is the author of *The Rebel Within, The Rebel Trap,* and *Rebels Divided,* three books in the Rebel series. In those stories, he explores the consequences of following conscience for those coming of age. He authored the Regina Shen series—*Regina Shen: Resilience, Regina Shen: Vigilance,* and *Regina Shen: Defiance.* This series takes place after abrupt climate change leads to the Great Collapse and a new society under the World Federation.

Find out more about the author and his work at LanceErlick.com. Go to that website to sign up to receive occasional email newsletters with links to free short stories, and updates on new releases and other writing developments.

www.ingramcontent.com/pod-product-compliance
Lightning Source LLC
Chambersburg PA
CBHW071258130626
46556CB00003B/1366